PRAISE FOR *BLUE NIGHT*

'If Philip Marlowe and Bernie Gunther got together in a Hamburg speakeasy and had a literary love child, then that might just explain Chastity Riley – Simone Buchholz's tough, acerbic and utterly engaging central character' William Ryan, author of *The Constant Soldier*

'A must-read, stylish and highly original take on the detective novel, written with great skill and popping with great characters' Judith O'Reilly, author of *Killing State*

'Simone Buchholz's witty and original *Blue Night*, beautifully translated by Rachel Ward, introduces us to maverick state prosecutor Chas Riley. Assigned the case of a badly beaten man, she embarks on a gripping investigation that's also a moving love letter to Hamburg and the bonds of friendship' Dr Kat Hall, author of *Der Krimi: Crime Fiction in German*

'*Blue Night* has great sparkling energy, humour and stylistic verve … and the story itself is gripping and pacey. Simone Buchholz's homage to Raymond Chandler and Jonny Cash is affectionate and deliberate. Then there's the interplay of author and translator, like musicians in the same band … creating an all-female tour de force' Rosie Goldsmith, European Literature Network

'*Blue Night* hits hard from page one with its beautifully atmospheric noir feel and a divisive, engaging main character in Chastity Riley – one to watch' Liz Loves Books

'A smashing thriller … highly recommended' *Reise Travel*

'Buchholz gives us a declaration of love for all the grime of a city of contrasts. Dripping with local colour, soaked in beer and infused with cigarette smoke, this is not your typical police procedural' Katy Derbyshire, Love German Books

'Not a word out of place – memorable characters – an absolute treat!' Michael J. Malone, author of *A Suitable Lie*

'The nonchalant, concise tone that's never too chummy nor too flippant or fixated on punchlines makes the story charming and interesting' *Frankfurter Allgemeine Zeitung*

'Chastity Riley belongs amongst Germany's most complex crime heroines: a lone wolf who looks into the chasms of human society' *Brigitte*

'Simone Buchholz just writes very, very well, all the while sure of her milieu, atmospherically confident and full of empathy for her characters' *Bücher magazin*

'Had me in its clutches from the very beginning. Exciting, unique and highly more-ish' The Writing Garnet

'A truly fresh narrative style which slowly lays out an intriguing and complex story. Chastity Riley is a unique and ultimately likeable character in a richly drawn world of vice' Jen Med's Book Reviews

'Explosive writing, larger-than-life characters, a killer mystery … Loved it!' LV Hay, author of *The Other Twin*

'Incredibly refreshing … with a fabulous cast of characters and a delicious sense of humour that won me over within the first few pages' NovelDeelights Blog

'I don't know how Chastity Riley does it … A woman who has plenty of compassion, and is loyal, funny and down to earth. A woman who has some of the best observations on life that I have read in fiction' Steph's Book Blog

BLUE NIGHT

ABOUT THE AUTHOR

Simone Buchholz was born in Hanau in 1972. At university, she studied philosophy and literature, worked as a waitress and a columnist, and trained to be a journalist at the prestigious Henri-Nannen-School in Hamburg. In 2016, Simone Buchholz was awarded the Crime Cologne Award as well as second place in the German Crime Fiction Prize for *Blue Night*, which was number one on the KrimiZEIT Best of Crime List for months. She lives in Sankt Pauli, in the heart of Hamburg, with her husband and son.

Follow Simone on Twitter @ohneKlippo and visit her website: *simonebuchholz.com*.

ABOUT THE TRANSLATOR

Rachel Ward is a freelance translator of literary and creative texts from German and French to English. Having always been an avid reader and enjoyed word games and puzzles, she discovered a flair for languages at school and went on to study modern languages at the University of East Anglia. She spent the third year working as a language assistant at two grammar schools in Saarbrücken, Germany. During her final year, she realised that she wanted to put these skills and passions to use professionally and applied for UEA's MA in Literary Translation, which she completed in 2002. Her published translations include *Traitor* by Gudrun Pausewang and *Red Rage* by Brigitte Blobel, and she is a Member of the Institute of Translation and Interpreting.

Follow Rachel on Twitter @FwdTranslations, on her blog *www.adiscounttickettoeverywhere.wordpress.com*, and on her website: *www.forwardtranslations.co.uk*.

BLUE NIGHT

SIMONE BUCHHOLZ

translated by Rachel Ward

**ORENDA
BOOKS**

Orenda Books
16 Carson Road
West Dulwich
London SE21 8HU
www.orendabooks.co.uk

First published in German as *Blaue Nacht* by Suhrkamp Verlag AG, Berlin 2016
This edition published in the United Kingdom by Orenda Books 2018
Copyright © Suhrkamp Verlag Berlin 2016
English translation © Rachel Ward 2017

ISBN 978-1-912374-01-4
eISBN 978-1-912374-02-1

Typeset in Garamond by MacGuru Ltd
Printed and bound by CPI Group (UK) Ltd, Croydon CR0 4YY

The translation of this work was supported by a
grant from the Goethe-Institut London

For sales and distribution, please contact *info@orendabooks.co.uk*.

For Rocco Willem Bruno

'I had my favourite easy chair right near the elevator and smoked my cigar. When I got sleepy, I retired to the Missing Persons office for a little snooze, leaving word with the cop at the information desk not to disturb me unless something really hot came over the teletype'

—Weegee (Arthur Fellig), police photographer in
New York from the 1930s to the 1960s.

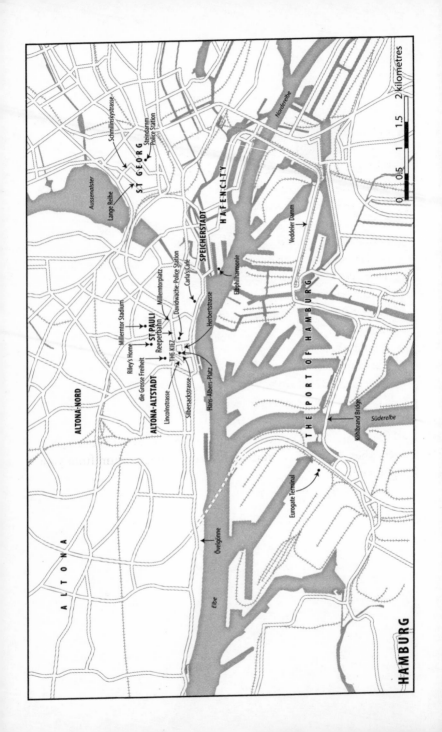

A kick in the right kidney brings you to your knees.

A kick in the belly, and you go down.

Kidneys again, left one this time, to really shut you up.

Then they whip the coshes out from under their jackets.

Three jackets, three coshes.

Left leg, right leg.

Left arm, right arm.

And six feet for twelve pairs of ribs.

Your very own many-headed demon.

Tailor-made to order.

Then out come the pliers.

Right index finger.

A clean crack.

But you're left-handed; they don't know everything.

One final kick to something broken.

Then they leave you lying there.

It took one minute, maybe two.

The pain is clear and confusing and hot and cold all at once and everywhere; your blood runs almost comfortingly warm from your right hand.

So this is what it's like.

CANDLES ALL ROUND, PLEASE

Under a dark sky the engine gives one last cough, clears its throat like an old man, then floods.

I get out, sit on the rusty-gold bonnet and raise my face to the heavy, cold air.

Cigarette.

First things first: I'm going to smoke this damn fog dry.

A weekend in the country: bullshit.

What was I thinking? It was a bloody stupid idea in the first place. So much for get yourself a car, get yourself out, have a change of scenery.

Bloody marvellous.

The car's a heap of junk and my driving's worse than a cow on ice. Which means, if I want to drive anywhere, nobody will come with me. So there's nobody but me. I can deal with that in town – better than anywhere else, anyhow. Driving through the countryside alone is like eating Sellotape.

Someone's waiting for me in town – I'm finally needed again – but now I'm trapped out here. Of course, the guy who's waiting for me doesn't know that he's waiting for me, because he's lying in hospital, smashed to bits. They called me because they always call me in cases like this.

They haven't called anyone else, because they don't know who he is.

I phone Faller, thanking God we still know each other. Nothing's happened yet that could have forced us apart.

He answers after the second ring. 'Good morning, my girl.'

'Good morning, Faller.'

'Well?'

'The Ford's dead.'

'Oh.'

'Can you pick me up, please? I need to get into town – urgently.'

'Where are you then?'

'In the middle of fucking nowhere,' I say.

'Where exactly?'

'Mecklenburg. Between Zarrentin and Wherethehellever. Somewhere on the B195, north of the motorway.'

'Aha.'

He's in the west of Hamburg, having breakfast probably. He could be here in an hour or so, if he puts his foot down.

'Don't go anywhere,' he says. 'I'll be there. Might take a while though.'

'I've got cigarettes. Call me when you get close, yeah?'

I hang up and grab the bonnet with both hands – it's already nearly cold. We've just never hit it off, this old car and me. Maybe it looked pretty good at first, maybe there was a superficial spark, maybe you could have been forgiven for thinking: genius! Why didn't anyone think of getting those two together! But in the end it was just one of those briefly exciting bar encounters, the kind that don't last ten sentences on closer inspection, and definitely not in daylight.

I turn up my coat collar, grab my bag from the boot and start walking down the road. Heading west. A vast landscape lies ahead of me: farmland and meadows and fields and a few isolated trees – a bit of ochre here, a bit of green there. I light my next cigarette and listen to my boots. We soon find a rhythm; we like walking on asphalt, my boots and me.

Faller will find me.

Behind me to the east, behind the wet, grim clouds and a long way away in this uniquely big Mecklenburg sky, there's a miserable scrap of morning sun.

I feel like a cowboy whose horse has been shot.

*

Faller's currently going through some kind of belated midlife crisis. I still can't believe he's bought a Pontiac. Sky blue, Catalina model, from the seventies. When he started spending more and more time openly checking out pretty young things his wife asked him if he wouldn't mind getting himself an unsuitable car instead. In fact, to put it another way, when he started claiming that the pretty young things were checking him out, his wife told him, 'You need something to do.'

And he's got that now – the Pontiac's always broken down. I'm in luck that his banger happens to be running just when mine isn't. 'Cos who the hell else could I have called?

Calabretta's got a big sign up saying *No Servizio*; it's nailed to his heart. I couldn't have dealt with that kind of misery this morning.

Klatsche will still be asleep. And he will have been behind the bar until just a few hours ago, so even if he were awake I couldn't assume he'd be able to drive.

And then there are Carla and Rocco. But they don't have a driving licence between them, and anyway, they're still officially on Calabretta-watch.

Seems me and my friends are a pretty immobile bunch.

He drives up slowly beside me, the Pontiac spluttering. He stops and rolls down the passenger window.

'I said to stay where you were.'

'Couldn't help it,' I say.

'But apart from that? Have a good weekend?'

I open the door, chuck my bag into the back seat and drop onto the black leather.

'Fantastic. That was definitely my last bloody trip out into the bloody country.'

He looks at me and shakes his head. 'Why do you do these things, Chastity? Just take off out of town? You need your concrete.'

What do I know? I thought I'd listen to my friends for once. Something had to give. All that sitting around just isn't for me. Since the business at the port, I'm still officially a public prosecutor, but unofficially I'm sidelined. They took a long time fretting over what to do with me. From the outside you'd imagine accusing your boss of corruption would get you promoted, but it's not looked on so kindly within the service.

And then there was the unauthorised use of firearms.

Having saved Calabretta's life is one thing; having shot a loser in the crown jewels instead of the leg is quite another. I don't know what happened to the guy after that; I never heard another word about it, and there wasn't even a murmur in the press. No idea how they wangled that, and I don't want to know either. They assured me that I had nothing to fear – just swiped my dad's army pistol and took me out of circulation for a while. And then, after months and months in the arse-end of nowhere, up they popped with the offer of a new job. A position created specially for me: victim protection.

If anyone gets half killed in a beating or a shooting or a hit-and-run anywhere in Hamburg, if anyone gets pushed off a bridge or a building and survives, it comes under my jurisdiction.

But only the victim, not the investigation.

Thrilling job.

Let me through, I'm here to hold his hand.

For the first few weeks, I stayed out of sight like a good girl and did as I was told. I've widened my horizons since then. Now I get a firm grip on the few cases that fall at my feet, even if that wasn't really the plan. Nobody's said anything yet though. What could they say? We're all in the same boat, after all, and the boat's called 'the good ship *Let's Just Not Make a Fuss about the Bloke with No Balls*'.

So there you are.

All things considered, no wonder I'm not wild about my temporary role.

All things considered, I was going stir-crazy.

Hence the crackpot idea of going away.

'Where to, then?' Faller does his taxi-driver voice. 'Home?'

'I've got to go to St Georg. To the hospital.'

'Aha,' he says, 'new patient.'

'New client,' I say.

'What about your car?'

'Let it make someone else happy.'

He accelerates and the Pontiac roars under my arse. It's a bit like driving a tank.

Always follow your heart. Or bury it at Wounded Knee.

My dad liked to trot that one out whenever I asked him what I should do. An old Native American proverb, I guess. Those boys had a snappy one-liner for every situation.

My heart says: Sit down and hold his hand. He doesn't look as though he's got anyone else to do it. I can recognise a lonely face from ten miles off.

The hand is warm and dry, and surprisingly soft for its size – it's a proper paw. I try to put both my hands round it. Ridiculous.

He was brought to the ward in the early morning, just after four. There are multiple fractures to his arms, legs and ribs; his right clavicle is smashed. There's a thick bandage round his right hand. The nurse says he's lost his index finger, but you can't just lose an index finger. He has no head injuries and his lungs aren't damaged. His kidneys are swollen but basically working. There's a single main doorway in his neck. That's where the drugs go in – the glittering disco stuff from the bags hanging on the drip stands. He's getting something to make him sleep and presumably all kinds of stuff for all kinds of pain. It's clearly working 'cos he looks strangely peaceful, and his face is unscathed, apart from a few scratches from the asphalt.

Forensics took his clothes; he had no papers on him.

He's really tall: with all the splints on his arms and legs he hardly fits the hospital bed. His hair shines silver-grey and it's close-cropped at the sides, a bit longer on top. His face is one of those angular models that men only grow into at a certain age. I'd put him at early-to-mid fifties. A man in his prime, if he weren't so broken.

Yeah, if he weren't so broken, he'd look a bit like a tall George Clooney.

The machines on the wall behind his bed start beeping. The nurse comes in and presses a few buttons. She smiles sympathetically around the room, as if I were a relative, even though she knows I'm not.

That keeps happening to me.

I don't always react to it very well.

'What was he wearing?' I ask her. 'Before the gown, I mean?'

She switches off her smile, question marks blinking dully in her eyes.

OK. Sorry.

'Where was he found?'

'I don't know exactly,' she says. 'Somewhere near here.'

Her stare is getting harder.

She seems to resent me: even if I'm not a relative, I could at least act like one.

She idly moves a few things from one side of the bed to the other, then hastily leaves the room before I can ask any more impudent questions.

I stay beside the tall, sleeping man and look at him.

I stay by him until the clouds finally seize power in the sky and it grows gradually dark; then I head home.

As I get out of the taxi in my road, cold rain falls on my head.

Yellow light rolls from Klatsche's window.

He's standing in the kitchen, making us cheese sandwiches; I'm sitting on the living-room floor watching two bottles of beer to stop them getting warm. We've turned the lights off and lit the candles. Klatsche started doing this a few years ago. A candle for each of us who needs it. Right now there are three: one for Calabretta, one for me, and one for Klatsche's gran. She's lying in bed in a care home in north Hamburg, with no idea what's what. At night they strap her down because she keeps wanting to run to the Moorweide bunker to get away from the bombs.

I never had a grandmother.

'Maybe we could start skipping my candle,' I say.

He stands beside me at the window with the plate of sandwiches. He's put gherkins on the cheese.

'Can you open the beer?' he asks. He says nothing about my candle.

'I don't need it any more.'

'The beer?'

'The candle. I'm fine.'

'Sure,' he says.

We clink glasses and drink, then we bite into the sandwiches.

'What's our Italian friend up to?' he asks, chews twice, swallows, next bite, big one. Big bloke, big appetite.

'I rang Carla yesterday,' I say. 'Calabretta was watching sport on TV. Before that he spent the day on the sofa, but without a blanket. He even answered occasionally if she asked him something. And he ate a plate of pasta. Carla reckons he's starting to pull himself together.'

'Rocco says he looks awful.'

'No wonder,' I say, biting into a slice of bread and cheese. It tastes rich and deep. The gherkin crunches between my teeth. A good cheese sandwich can save lives, I'm convinced of that.

Calabretta had actually tried his luck with Betty, our elegant pathologist. She'd given him the cold shoulder a couple of times in the last few years, probably because he'd acted like an idiot. In matters of the heart, Calabretta's as big a loser as I am. But this time she'd gone with it, for whatever reason. And then it had actually worked out between them; maybe it was the stars, or the moon, or the harbour air, or maybe Betty had just gone soft. They'd been glued to each other for a whole year – he was at home with her, and she with him and everything was full of happiness. There was something almost creepy about it – as if they'd ordered the sun to takeaway. But then, overnight, Betty switched to a better sun, at a forensic medicine conference in Munich. A Swiss professor. She chucked in her life in Hamburg. And Calabretta.

That was last winter, and since then he's been black inside.

We drink beer.

I mention that I was at the hospital and what was going on.

'You don't know who the guy is?' asks Klatsche.

'Nope. And nobody seems to be missing him yet.'

'What are you planning to do?' he asks.

Do my job, I think. I say: 'Have a look at his stuff. And sit by his bed and wait for him to wake up.'

'Is he under guard?' asks Klatsche. He's a street kid. He hasn't lost the instinct for when someone's in danger. His bristly hair pricks up like antennae; his green eyes have snapped to attention.

'I don't know why he was beaten up, but there's always a policeman sitting outside his door,' I say.

Klatsche nods, settles his antennae again, swigs his beer and says: 'Should we light a candle for him?'

1982, summer.

FALLER, GEORG

So two evenings a week, just before the cemetery shuts its gates, I go to visit Minou. There aren't many people about between the graves at that time. Only the old trees look at me. Branches nodding towards me now and again are quite enough company.

Nobody knows about me and Minou. My colleagues on the squad don't and nor do my two-and-a-half friends. Nobody knows that she had to die because I fell in love with her.

If you want a girl from the Kiez – the red-light district – and you're not her pimp, you have to pay him for her. I knew that, of course. But I thought nobody would notice.

It was almost nothing really. Whenever I saw her it was still under the heading of services offered. Nobody can look into people's hearts, can they? Or so I thought.

And suddenly she was dead.

The price that Minou had to pay for me wanting her.

They just shot her.

Come on, boy, girls in the Kiez are part of a business model. You knew that. So don't make such a fuss.

But I do make a fuss. I miss her. She's on my conscience. You can twist it how you like. I could bash my head through solid concrete for it.

When I stand by her grave, I drop to my knees. Whether I want to or not.

Sometimes, someone puts flowers on her plot.

It isn't me. I can't. I write her little notes and bury them.

And then I'm there at her grave, half kneeling, half curled in a ball, waiting for night to fall from the sky.

They won't do anything like that to me again.

Or to anyone who belongs to me.

The girl from Herbertstrasse and the love-sick cop.

Sounds like a shit story.

RILEY, CHASTITY

The last summer holiday before high school tears us apart. Some of us are going to one place, others are going to another.

The last summer before things get serious, says Dad.

As if it had been a barrel of laughs till now.

I wear cut-off jeans and Dad's old army shirts and sometimes clogs. Mostly I go barefoot. I like the warm streets under my feet. I like needing to be careful.

We play James Bond on the banks of the Main. The boys want to play James Bond. Or we play World War II. Then we ride through Sachsenhausen on our folding bikes. Germans versus the Allies.

I'm always the Americans.

Of course.

The boys go nuts for Dad's army shirts.

We play war or James Bond till the sun ducks behind the houses.

All of Frankfurt glows gold and orange and pink. It comes from the red sandstone that they built the city from.

At night in bed I think that sometimes I'd like a girl friend, but I don't know how to get one. And I think that I'd like a mother – a mother who's here, that is; here with me. Really, I want my mum.

Every evening I think about her and ask myself over and over again how she could do that, just go off. And Dad stands outside my door and sheds secret tears for me and my childhood and our broken family. And I act like I don't notice, and try to damn well pull myself together again.

He really can't help it.

She just wanted to get away. Out of the country bombed by the war when she was a kid.

And then this man – this other officer – took her with him.
That's what I tell myself. In bed at night.
Dad really can't help it.
But he still thinks it's all his own fault.

KLASSMAN, HENRI

I hadn't even been born. So I've got nothing to say.

Perhaps my mum had just met my dad. Whoever he was.

I do know one thing: my mum wanted a son called Henri. Because of all the sailors she used to know.

CALABRETTA, VITO

Through the streets of Altona. Alone.

I like running around alone. I run to and fro and to and fro. And whenever I go past my parents' *supermercato*, I pop in.

It sucks me in, the shop. Because an Italian can't walk past his family, says my dad.

But I don't like to stay long. I usually go straight out again. It's cold in the shop. The chiller's too big.

And if my mum catches me, I have to sort things. Into boxes, out of boxes, in and out. I hate sorting boxes.

It's not complicated or anything, but it makes me crazy. Because it seems so pointless. As if I only have to do it so I'll stay in the shop. So I won't run around outside.

But running around outside is the only thing that untangles my brain. When I'm running around outside I can cope.

It's my way of sorting things, I tell my mum.

She doesn't understand. She wants me to sort the boxes.

VELOSA, CARLA

Early morning at Grandma's in Lisbon. Down in the Alfama.

She beats octopuses against the wall. As many as she can, she beats against the wall.

It softens the brutes up, she says.

My grandpa caught them. The octopuses.

But me too, says Grandma.

Later, Grandpa sells everything at the fish market.

But not Grandma, he says.

The wall next to the door to my grandparents' ground-floor flat is all black. From all the ink.

Soon, when I go to school and finally learn to read and write, I'll pinch a bit of ink, then I'll write things on the road.

The sky over the Tejo is purple and red. From all the octopus souls, says Grandma.

Is the sky a different colour everywhere in the world?

Yes, says Grandma, because it depends who is dying under that sky.

MALUTKI, ROCCO

My mum is the most beautiful hooker of all. Not just in St Pauli. In the whole world.

She has the biggest and most beautiful boobs in the whole world.

My dad played the violin in an orchestra. Nobody knows where he is now, but that's not so bad, says Mum.

She says: Some people weren't meant to stay put.

We manage just fine as it is. Fresh money comes in every night.

In the morning, when she gets in from work, she stands at the ironing board and irons the money.

There, she says, when she's finished and has folded up the board, now it's clean again.

JOE

Hey.

Hamburg.

ONLY THE ROAD (AND ABOVE IT THE PRETTY LIGHTS)

Watch out.

Early-rising day in the Klatsche household.

The Blue Night is shut on Mondays and the boss goes shopping. Schnapps, pretzels, butter, liquorice. Then in the mornings, there's the beer delivery. Bottled beer. Klatsche had draught beer poisoning a few years ago. Badly cleaned beer lines. It happens, I said at the time.

'Not at my place,' he said when he took over from fat, old Ali at the Blue Night.

So there's been a sign hanging over the bar ever since:

'DRINK WITH CONFIDENCE
NO DRAUGHT BEER POISONING HERE – GUARANTEED'

He brings me a coffee in bed, drops a kiss on my brow.

What a lovely alarm clock.

Then he's gone.

I get up and gather my clothes from last night. My jumper's in the living room, right next to the window sill, my jeans too. My underwear is somewhere else entirely. He always does that. I put some clothes on and go over to my flat to shower. I take the coffee with me.

Later, in the taxi, the city slips past the corners of my eyes. It's like somebody intentionally thought up the dirty grey of advanced February but then just spewed it out instead of putting their heart into it. Outside, it's so sunless the streetlamps are on the point of coming on but not quite dark enough for them to make it.

A lousy fake of a day.

The suit feels heavy and black in my hands. Expensive fabric, no label. Clearly made to measure. The black shirt is a British brand, the shoes come from the USA.

The walls around me are light grey and they glisten. The smooth lino under my feet swallows up every sound and every odour; the neon light absorbs all warmth.

I'd almost like some company.

It's always the same when I hold this kind of thing in my hands: clothes, or a murder weapon, or some bloodstained item from a person who didn't get out of an incident in one piece. I think that these things ought to tell me a bit about what happened. As if objects have a memory. But as always there's only a feeling. This time it's:

It wasn't a surprise.

I put everything back in the plastic wrappers, take off the gloves and thank my colleagues from forensics, hunched over a couple of microscopes in the room next door. Then I get into the lift at the end of the corridor and go up a couple of floors to have a closer look at Calabretta.

Once I went in and out of police headquarters all the time. Now I avoid coming here. Because it makes me feel watched. A few years ago I couldn't shake off the feeling that I was screeching round the bends all the time, but really I was going dead straight compared to the lurching zigzag of my current life.

Calabretta looks like shit, of course, but at least he's more than just physically present now. I can actually make out signs of life in his eyes. In the first few weeks after he and Betty split up, they were just two glowering holes, scattering darkness, and not entirely belonging to the body curled in a foetal position under the blankets on Carla and Rocco's couch.

But something seems to have happened since Saturday. Carla hinted as much.

At least Calabretta's no longer lying on that couch. Calabretta's sitting at his desk and tapping at his computer keyboard. When he spots me, he looks up.

I lean against the wall opposite him. 'Well?'

'Nice to see you,' he says.

'Nice to see *you*,' I say.

He breathes in deeply, and out again, and looks out of the window.

Ah. End of conversation. In my imagination, I can hear the half-fossilised heart in his chest. It's trying to knock on the walls, to send a signal perhaps, but nothing's coming through properly.

He starts typing again.

I look at him a bit longer, but there's no further reaction. I head into the room next door, to my colleagues Schulle and Brückner.

'Hey, boss.'

'Mornin' boss!'

'Hello gentlemen. I'm not your boss any more. Remember?'

'Don't matter, boss.'

'Yeah, fuck 'em.'

I like these two so much that I could buy them an ice cream every time I see them.

'How's business?' I ask, sitting on the ripped, black leather sofa in the corner.

'Fine,' says Schulle. 'We're watching a guy who's probably taken out his wife, but we're still looking for the body.'

'Are you still looking after your depressive colleague?' I ask quietly.

'*Naturalmente*,' says Brückner.

'Does he go out with you now and again?'

'Jesus!'

They slap their thighs as if I've asked if they've heard the rumour that the moon's been seen wearing ears and a false nose.

Schmilinskystrasse. Right on the border between the squalor behind the station and the elegant surroundings of the Aussenalster Lake.

A white turn-of-the-century house; the ground floor façade's painted grey and merges almost seamlessly with the asphalt. Two trees stick out of the pavement right and left of the door, their bare branches stretching towards the sky. Ghostly fingers. Across the road is a tree hung all over with fairy lights; its suggestion of homeliness strikes me as no less spooky.

They found the man here. He was lying on the pavement, his broken arms and legs at unusual angles to his body; he'd probably fainted from all the blood flowing from the wound on his right hand, as well as the pain in the rest of his body.

The blood has gone now. They've been and scrubbed it away, as fast as ever. Now things look almost like they did forty-eight hours ago, before he was beaten to a pulp on Saturday night. All you can see is a large, faint stain; all that distinguishes the cleaned grey from the rest of the grey is its slightly chemical nature. The colour doesn't smell of the street.

I stand on the steps by the front door and sigh at the pavement. Look left and right along the road.

One man?

Hardly.

A gang attack?

More likely.

I look up at the façades; people live here, although not many – most of the flats are offices now. If you attack someone here you want things to quieten down quickly because it's always quiet here the rest of the time. You want things short and sweet. Not too much of a struggle. So you'd do better as part of a group. Besides, the man in the hospital is too tall and broad-shouldered for a single attacker. There must have been at least two of them, if not three or even four.

I pull a Lucky from the box and light up. Where did they come from? From all sides, I think. And then they left him lying outside the house. I scan down the doorbells and note the names. There are people with names like bad weather: Rainier and Fogdt. And then they shack up together.

'He woke up briefly last night,' says a doctor who looks barely seventeen. 'Spoke to the nurse on duty.'

'What did he say?' I ask.

'He said: "It takes over from everything you love."'

'Sorry?'

'"It takes over from everything you love."'

'Nothing else?'

'Nothing else.'

The teenage doctor is standing by the man's bed, looking at him, his hands in his pockets. His white coat hangs loose on his body; he wears it like a trench coat.

I sit down on the man's bed and look at him. Between his eyes is a frown line that wasn't there yesterday. He doesn't look peaceful any more. You could say that he looks a little dangerous.

'How is he?' I ask.

'He'll need a lot of physio,' says the doctor. 'And he's not a young man any more. With all those broken bones … it might be a while before he can walk again.'

'I mean, how's he doing *now*?'

'His body has got over the initial shock quite well. Everything's doing its job. We'll gradually phase out the soporifics.'

'But he's still on painkillers…?'

The seventeen-year-old says, 'Of course.' He frowns and stares at me, and his look says: Do you take me for an idiot?

I give him five of my cards and say: 'I'd like you to put them up in the nurses' station and on all the toilet mirrors. I want one of you to call me right away if he wakes up, even at night.' My look says: Or there'll be trouble, kid.

He gets it and departs in official silence. If he weren't even younger than Klatsche, I'd go out for a beer with him like a shot.

I watch the child-doctor for a moment longer through the closed door, then I take the hand of the man I'm responsible for. Dry and warm. Unchanged.

We sit like that for a long time. Outside, someone – the late winter or the early spring or just the north – is whistling a quirky tune. The wind at hospital windows sounds different from a breeze swinging past a cinema, for example. Or a café. There's something comfortable about an outdoor sound like that. Maybe you pull your collar a bit tighter and hunch your shoulders a little, and then you sigh and feel cosy and happy that you're wherever you happen to be. The wind at hospital windows, on the other hand, inspires yearning. Although you know that the wind out there would only whistle in your face – and you must be too weak for that or you wouldn't be in here, would you? – there's nothing you'd rather do than get out and into the whistling.

The man suddenly takes two rather deeper breaths and winces as he breathes out again. Something tells me that he'll wake up tomorrow morning.

I pick up a water glass from the window sill, hold it over my mouth, wheeze into the glass and whisper: 'Luke, I am your father.'

Classic displacement activity.

As I leave the hospital, the day's clocking off too. A deep sigh falls over the city. The streetlights now have a right to be on and the asphalt relaxes. I walk along the Alster and the canals that take me to the port. Walking beside water always seems so much easier than taking some road. The water moves with me, sweeps me along.

And sweeps out my messed-up head.

The windows in Carla's café are fogged up, the chandelier and candles are lit. The place is like a perpetual Christmas tree, shining tirelessly on the concrete outside the windows.

The door opens; two guys in woolly hats come out. They nod to me and I let myself be drawn in by the warmth.

Carla threads her way through the tables in her high heels, serving up steaming plates of food. She's wearing a tight black dress with a neckline as deep as the harbour basin, her long, dark curls tumbling down her back. She twinkles at me and blows a kiss across the room. Rocco is standing in the tiny, still-improvised kitchen right behind the bar. He's busy with pans, pots and plates, his disorganised hair flying out behind him, followed by tiny droplets of sweat. His performance looks like a cross between *Flashdance* and the *Muppet Show* chef. He's got no time for anything. The kitchen's too tense and too crowded even for the heat, so it comes to stretch and settle down out here with us. Inspector Calabretta is sitting at the bar, drinking beer. He's wearing the same grey jumper and jeans as this morning, his once-black hair is greying nicely; slicked back this morning, it's come loose over the day and wavy strands have fallen into his face. He just needs a fag in the corner of his mouth, a hand raised to heaven, a twist of the hips, and it's a perfect Celentano impression. Seeing him sit there like that, I realise he's lost weight. Not the slightest hint of a belly, not anywhere. Broken heart, cold kitchen. Poor bloke. I sit next to him, look at him. He doesn't look back.

Carla slips behind the counter, glances at Calabretta and shrugs. 'You want a beer too, darling? If you want to match your neighbour you've got some catching up to do.'

'Yes,' I say, 'I'd like a beer too, please.' And I put a hand on Calabretta's forearm. 'What are two pretty things like us going to get up to this evening, eh?'

He turns to face me, looks at me, eyes full of nothing. Then he looks back at his half-full bottle of beer and I can tell from his expression that right now, for him, every bottle is definitely half empty and not half full. Carla passes me my beer and we clink bottles. She's grabbed herself a *knolle*, a stubby bottle of Astra, from the fridge, which means it's about an hour till closing time. I show my Italian pal how fast I can drink then put my bottle down next to his.

'Snap,' I say.

'If you've just secretly emptied three more, then yeah,' he says.

There it is again: empty.

I let my head drop onto the bar; it doesn't hurt. I lift my head again and we sit side by side in silence for two more beers. The people at the tables begin to ask for their bills, Carla starts polishing glasses, and I turn to Calabretta:

'Have you eaten anything?'

He shakes his head.

Rocco comes out of the kitchen, strokes his hair out of his eyes and then wipes his greasy hands on a towel.

Looks like someone needs a bath this evening.

'Can we still get something to eat?' I ask.

Rocco pulls a tired, stressed face.

Since the two of them turned the café into a daytime restaurant, both the owners' skills and the kitchen capacity have been permanently overwhelmed. But they cope and the place is buzzing.

'Just something quick and easy,' I say.

'Sure,' says Rocco with a forgiving smile as he vanishes into the kitchen, coming back a few minutes later with two serious sandwiches: one ham and mozzarella, one mozzarella and parsley. The rolls are warm. He wraps them in thick paper.

'Thanks,' I say, leaving a twenty on the bar for everything, before Calabretta and I vanish into the night, while Carla and Rocco set to work rounding off the day and the mayhem.

Riley, you take over.

''S good to walk a bit,' says Calabretta. He's dug his hands deep into the pockets of his brown leather jacket.

We walk down the glittering Reeperbahn. On a cold Monday evening the place is dead. All shut, nobody at the ready. Not even the homeless. They headed for the city's less draughty corners, or even the emergency shelters, at the beginning of winter. They'll be back in late April, early May. Only our boots clatter over the cobbles.

There's only the road.

And above it the pretty lights.

Below them is the memory of the weekend, when there was singing and dancing, when there was kissing and whooping and beating into the early hours, like there's been on this stage for more than a hundred years. Places notice these things and hold onto them.

Now and again a couple of tourists come towards us, wondering as much about the scenery as about themselves. They feel instinctively that this isn't their night. We turn right, then left and right again, and we're back at a bar. We drink an arsenal of long drinks. Cuba libre for Calabretta, vodka and tonic for me. The outline of a guitar-playing cowboy shines in the window in blood red and citrus orange and late-summer yellow; the bass from the speakers over the bar smacks me in the gut. There needs to be more smoking. That's what I want to say, the way you have to say that kind of thing when you get a phrase on the tip of your tongue after three beers and four vodkas, but all I can get over my lips is the 'more', and the cigarette just makes it into my mouth, whereas something comes over Calabretta, as it so often does when you drink a lot for a long time: he's flooded with a sudden clarity.

'There's a problem with Faller,' he says.

'What problem?'

I can't make anything of his speech. Nothing.

'He's getting more and more restless,' says Calabretta.

Oh, right.

'Oh, right,' I say. 'He's having … a … thing … midlife crisis … you know…'

'I don't mean that,' says Calabretta. 'Although that might be part of it.'

A sudden whistle goes off in my head.

'I think,' he says, 'he wants another go at the Albanian. He wants to do something himself – take action, you see? He's said stuff like that recently, more than once. He's planning something. But I've got no idea what it could be.'

And I've got no idea where Calabretta's suddenly getting all these words from.

I look at him. His eyes spin before my eyes, and I feel the information spilling out of my ears; it hasn't even made it as far as my brain; the only thing that sticks is a difficult feeling. I pull my colleague down from his barstool, haul him out onto the street and then on to the next bar. I put him down next to me and order two aquavits.

'Ah,' he says. 'Linie.'

1987, autumn.

FALLER, GEORG

Homicide squad. I'm new here.

And spending more time in the red-light district than ever.

There've been so many deaths since coke hit the Kiez.

First the pimps snort holes through their noses, then they shoot holes through the other pimps' faces.

The gangs and bosses are new too. They speak Turkish or Kurdish or Lebanese.

We don't understand their language. We don't understand what they do. Or how they do it.

A colleague always says: Shit, they're wired differently from Hein and Klaus and Johnny.

I say: Calm down. We're still getting to grips with them. We just need to get deeper into the business.

RILEY, CHASTITY

Everyone keeps falling in love now.

What's that all about?

CALABRETTA, VITO

Mum cries in Italian. She cries loud and she cries a lot.

Because Dad's a womaniser, she says.

I hold her hand and then we smoke Aldi cigarettes together.

VELOSA, CARLA

We're not in Lisbon any more.

Only Grandma stayed in Portugal.

She didn't want to go anywhere any more. She didn't want to come to Hamburg. She wasn't going anywhere without Grandpa, she said. And Grandpa can't go anywhere, because Grandpa's in the cemetery.

My parents wanted to come here even though no one hits octopuses against the walls by this harbour.

Here, the wind hits you in the face. But from my parents' restaurant I can see and hear the ships. I like them.

And the gulls.

First thing in the morning, when Mum and Dad head for the kitchen to prepare the fish and peel the potatoes, Dad gets out his *fado* records and the sound fills the whole restaurant.

The day starts like that, and the day stops like that. With songs of longing.

KLASSMAN, HENRI

I play with keys a lot.

Those plastic keys.

MALUTKI, ROCCO

My keys are metal ones. You can cut them to any shape you want. Then you really can get into anywhere.

Other things I can do:

A standing somersault.

A wicked BMX stunt.

Send a dead ball scorching down the pitch.

And that trick where you steal people's wallets on the train and they even thank you for it.

Don't you know that trick?

Well, I'll come round and show you then.

JOE

Nobody knows my name.

They only know my way of dancing with them. In the moment it happens. Quick and quiet.

I mostly work in St Pauli. My room's the other side of town. There's wallpaper with mountains and a cold lake in the middle.

WHAT THE FUCK DO YOU CARE HOW DARK IT IS OUTSIDE MY WINDOW?

I don't know what to do with the telephone. It's too loud.

It's got to stop.

I thrash around with my hand, raising my arm as far as I can, and try to find the thing. There. Left of my bed. That takes so long, a thought filters through to me: throwing the phone at the wall would not be good.

Answering it would be good.

Cough, breathe, hack. I feel dizzy. Lying down.

'Yes?' Oh God. My voice sounds like an old crow making a crash landing.

'St Georg Hospital here, surgical ward. Good morning. Am I speaking to Ms Riley?'

'Yes, I think so.'

'He's awake,' says the hospital voice, sounding a bit offended. 'You wanted us to call you immediately.'

'I did,' I say. 'What time is it?'

'Half past five.'

I see. No wonder I feel dizzy. I only went to bed three hours ago and not with particular aplomb. More of a stumble really. I think I can vaguely remember crashing into a door frame between the bathroom and bedroom. I feel my head. Right. There's a bump. I open my eyes a crack; the full moon glitters right in my face. Not a cloud in the sky.

Unusual for the time of year.

My current condition is not. Alcohol helps me through the winter. I was overjoyed when I was finally old enough to drink properly.

'Has he said anything?' I ask.

'No. He doesn't speak. He just looks at us strangely – sort of …
annoyed.'

'Hasn't he even asked where he is?'

'He seems perfectly aware of that.' The hospital voice is becoming
impatient.

'I'll come as soon as I can,' I say, although at the moment I'm not
quite sure if that'll even be today. 'If he speaks, will you please take
note of what he says?'

'I can't remember everything patients come out with.'

'Then bloody well write it down.'

I hang up and feel guilty. Firstly because I'm not sitting at the
beaten man's bedside, which is the only job I actually have at the
moment. And secondly, because I was rude to nursing staff, a dying
breed. I sit on the edge of the bed and realise that I shouldn't even
start thinking about the day without a serious batch of headache
pills.

I try to stand up and cling onto the wall.

Uh-huh.

Oh boy!

On the other side of the wall, Klatsche's asleep in bed. The wall
feels like one big heat pad. I go even wobblier at the knees and have
to watch myself or I'll fall on my face.

I could just lie back down again.

It seems like there are lots more white coats wandering around here
than usual. And they've picked up the pace. They zoom past on
either side of me, as if Old Nick himself was at their heels.

It's probably just a change of shift.

Day is breaking, even if there'll be only moonlight outside for
some time yet.

Ward B2, room 5. Outside the door is a chair, and sitting on the
chair is one of the officers posted to make sure that no one but me

and the hospital staff gets in. I give a tiny salute and show my pass; the policeman nods back. He looks tired. I reckon he's still the night shift, like me.

The man in room 5 is sitting up slightly in bed – the head end's been raised and a couple of pillows shoved under his neck, one flowered and another chequered. From the look of the pillows, nobody's been to shake them out for a while. They probably don't dare. The man looks like he might bite. It almost sounds like he's growling at me. When I actually have the nerve to step through the doorway into his room, he turns away and stares out of the window as if to say: She's all I need.

'It's still dark out there,' I say. 'What's so fascinating, apart from your own reflection?'

'What the fuck do you care how dark it is outside my window?' he asks.

He was more charming asleep.

He speaks with an accent, but I can't place it. I pull a chair up to his bed and sit down.

'I don't remember offering you a seat,' he says, and now he's clearly an Austrian.

'I'm not the type to wait for an invitation,' I say.

He's still looking out of the window.

'My name is Riley,' I say. 'I'm a public prosecutor and I take care of people like you.'

'People like me?'

He starts to laugh. It's not a crazy laugh; he seems genuinely amused. Then he looks at me for the first time. Blue eyes. Bright blue, forget-me-not eyes with a pale ring around the pupils. With his down-to-earth face they could make him look like an outdoorsy type, a guy who lives for the water or the mountains, but he's a touch too elegant for that. Something tells me he's rooted in civilisation. It's that George Clooney thing. Perhaps I just have the tailor-made suit on my mind, but it's got me a bit confused, and I don't know what to focus on. How to approach him. I need a clear message when

I'm getting to know someone. An unambiguous signal to heart and mind, an unmistakable clue about who I'm dealing with. Otherwise it's too complicated for me. I'm not very good at that stuff. When it comes to relationships, I'm an amateur.

'My job is to protect you,' I say, 'and to make sure that we catch the people who beat you up.'

Of course I know how corny that sounds, but like I said, it's hard for me. It's easy to end up sounding like a cop show.

'Bullshit,' he says. He glowers at me. 'What was your name?'

'Chastity Riley,' I say.

'Funny name.' Flawless Austrian accent.

'I know. I've learnt to live with it. And what's yours?'

His gaze strays back to the window; the dark blue in the sky is growing paler with every minute and the reflection of the room is starting to fade. The moon is still shining brightly and it's coming in through the window now.

'Pick something,' says the Austrian.

'Rumpelstiltskin?' I ask.

'Not bad.' A soft Austrian smile.

'You won't get rid of me that way,' I say.

He looks at me; no, he stares at me, and then he whispers: 'I'm Joe.'

'You're Austrian. Your name's not Joe.'

'Have you ever been to Austria? Skiing?' he asks.

I shake my head.

'You see,' he says. 'You've got no idea.'

'About skiing?'

'About everyday naming customs in the Alps.'

'OK,' I say, 'Joe. Who broke all your bones?'

'Life,' he says, shutting his eyes, turning his head away and acting like I'm not there. Seems he makes a habit of pathetic posturing. Seems our conversation's over.

There's no rational reason to feel like this, but it's pretty clear: I like this Alpine son of a bitch.

I stand up and say: 'I'll leave you in peace for today. But I'll be back.'

He frowns and deep wrinkles form on his brow.

'I can bring a couple of beers,' I say, already halfway out of the door.

As I close it behind me, I think I hear someone mumble, '*Prosit!*' but I'm not quite sure.

The policeman on the chair looks at me and says: 'You're brave.'

Clearly he's been in for a visit too.

It's light at last. A pale but bright sky. And, very slowly, my inner light bulbs are coming on. I walk a little way down Lange Reihe, the city's most colourful street. No two of the old townhouses are the same, and every one of them houses a café or a restaurant or a shop selling clothes or pots or chocolate or books or tea or gay porn or floor lamps, and often a bit of everything, over two floors where they can. And it seems like there are signs everywhere: *We kindly ask you to enter this world in as many colours and shapes as possible.*

But the street is still sleeping. And without its people, the brightly coloured road has lost its cheer.

It's hard at the best of times in a north-German port city in wrinkly March – laughing, I mean. The rest, i.e. everything you can do without laughing, is almost easier here than anywhere else. We just let ourselves fall into the mist and all the sad things run under their own steam. Loneliness, for example. Or fear. Or being cut off from everything. Things like that.

So he's an Austrian. Traditionally, Austrians up here are in one of two industries: publishing and the red-light business. No idea why that is, or who was the first to move north to work for a magazine or for a Reeperbahn boss, or to become one themselves. That's just the way it is.

The Austrian in the hospital looks like a big editorial beast, but acts like a big shot in the Kiez. Of course he *might* still work in a smart office, but people who don't want to give their names generally don't even trust themselves – not an inch. And people who mistrust themselves mistrust others. They have no friends. People don't know them. They don't join in with normal stuff. And if you don't join in, you're practically not there.

And then you're perfect for crime.

Klatsche always says: If you see a gangster, they're no good.

I think Klatsche quit his career as king of the burglars because he realised – in jail, if not before – that as a criminal he could crack safes but not hearts. And he loves doing the hearts. He tries it with me every day. I'd like to say he's biting on granite but that's not quite true. I'm more like toast in his hands: a bit chewy, but generally rather brittle.

Before Klatsche was Mr Barkeeper, back when he was the most popular locksmith in St Pauli, he tried out his skills on closed doors. Since he stopped doing that, he's been working on my locked-up soul. He thinks it's good for me. Carla thinks so too. I think there's nothing I can do about it.

Not being able to do anything about it reminds me of Calabretta and our wild night yesterday evening. I make a mental note: call Calabretta. Because there was something. Something he said was important, but I can't quite grasp it. I can feel it though – there's a dark patch on my brain, stuck on my thoughts like an exploded black felt-tip.

I flag down a taxi. Now I need coffee and cigarettes and a warm face. Somebody happy. I like sleepy places, but the empty Lange Reihe is doing me in. On top of the foul-mouthed Austrian in the hospital it's just a bit too much *UGH, NOT YOU* this early in the morning.

The taxi drives through the city and while the sun tiptoes surreptitiously past the clouds, while the knot in my head works tentatively looser, someone adds a soundtrack to my hangover, which until then I'd barely noticed. As I get out of the car outside Carla's café, there's something buzzing in my ear like an old David Lynch film. If you could put a punchy beat over it and sell it, it would go like hot cakes.

I stretch and my spine cracks. Someone desperately needs to go for a run again. That's the thing: when winter comes to an end, everything's a bit askew. I keep stretching on the pavement gym. It cracks again. I resolve to lace on my running shoes as soon as possible, and my hangover muscles through, adding fuel to my resolution; but then the door opens and Carla pops out and presses a thick glass mug of steaming latte into my hand and says she's put the sugar in already, and, whoops, everything's slid back to a whole lot more horizontal again. I light a cigarette to go with the coffee, puff little clouds into the air and relax, which is easy with Carla's place behind me.

Wonder where Faller is; I call him.

He doesn't answer, which never happens. I blink into the sun a bit longer as it reflects off the window opposite, accept the buzzing in my head as a given and go in to order another coffee.

I like my friend's café best in the mornings, when you'd never guess that it's a restaurant in the afternoons and evenings now. In the mornings, time slows down here – Carla's just too tired for stress before ten. She's getting everything set with careful movements that shift the air cautiously from here to there. The *fado* streams from the speakers as dark and soft as the coffee from the silver espresso machine; a slight smile billows through the room. Rocco is standing in the kitchen, beating eggs in a bowl. He looks freshly showered, almost freshly hatched – his hair is wet and shining and combed smoothly back. Only later in the day will the curls on his head assert themselves and start giving incomprehensible orders to the kitchen utensils stacked all around.

'Ah,' he says, beaming at me, 'the prosecution! It's about time justice put in an appearance round here.'

Carla is standing behind the bar now, moving glasses and plates from one place to another and back again.

'He feels unfairly treated,' she says, unleashing a meaningful glance.

'I don't *feel* unfairly treated,' says Rocco, 'I *am* unfairly treated. I have to spend every hour of the day standing in this kitchen. And when I'm finally allowed out and start looking forward to being with my wife, she's, and I quote, "too tired for everything". Every time.'

I sit down at the bar. Carla sees the dangerously low coffee level in my glass, points at it and asks: 'One for the road, right?'

I nod and turn to Rocco: 'Whose idea was the restaurant again?'

'Some guy,' he says. 'I've forgotten his name.'

'You see,' I say, 'we have too. Wait for the name to come back to you, and then complain to him. Can I have some scrambled eggs, please?'

He sighs and reaches for the heavens. 'What did I do to deserve this?'

'With mozzarella,' I say.

Rocco shakes his head, looks at me and says: 'You're nuts, Calamity Jane.'

'Riley,' I say. 'Chastity Riley.'

'Love you too,' he says, starting to make my scrambled eggs and cheese. Then he mumbles something about taxes, which he doesn't pay, but if he did, then he really bloody would.

Carla takes two cups of espresso to the table left of the window. She walks like a conquering hero.

Love is war, once you let yourself get sucked into it. Which is precisely why Klatsche and I won't be doing that. Well, I won't be.

'Well, my girl?'

Faller.

Suddenly standing next to me.

'I rang you a couple of minutes ago,' I say.

'Oh. I haven't got my phone on me.'

'Faller, you *always* have your phone on you. You're a cop.'

'I *was* a cop,' he says. 'Now I'm a man of private means. And on course to loosen up a bit.'

Loosen up? This old stickler?

'I don't think it'll suit you,' I say.

'Just you wait and see how relaxed I can get,' he says. 'You'll be in for a surprise.'

He lets Carla stroke his shoulder and give him a coffee. Americano, black, no sugar. He puts his hat and coat down on the stool next to him but keeps his scarf on.

I'll be in for a surprise? And then I remember what Calabretta was talking about yesterday evening – there was something wrong with my dear old colleague Faller. He was up to something. Something difficult. I still don't know exactly what it was about and, given how tentatively my system is recovering from the excesses of last night, I imagine there's not that much extra information lurking in my aching head.

'What are you up to, Faller?' I ask.

Faller blows on then sips at his hot coffee.

'Nothing. Why?' He looks indignantly at me. He really is up to something then.

'You just said I'll be in for a surprise, so I'm wondering what it'll be.'

'Me?' he says. 'Relaxed as hell and resplendent in all my glory.'

'Faller?'

'Yes?'

'I don't believe a word of it.'

'I'm devastated,' he says. 'We should have breakfast together to console me. We haven't done that for ages. What will you have?'

'Scrambled eggs,' I say. 'It's on its way.'

'If I order croissants and jam for both of us, can I have some of your eggs?' He lays his hand on my forearm and gives me one of those whatever-happens-I'm-on-your-side looks.

'Sure,' I say and postpone my investigation till later. That dad trick gets me every time.

We sit side by side, drinking coffee and eating scrambled eggs with jam croissants. Outside a few confused snowflakes tumble out of a properly bright sky. They're probably just as surprised as I am by this sudden light. Although you can't actually see the sun. It's probably just a shimmer left behind over the city from when it appeared for a moment. Some northern cities can do that. Put a little bit of sunshine aside so they can get it out later if they need it. It's an idea I could do with in my life. I glance sideways at Faller. He notices and grins, but doesn't look at me. I stop thinking about the mistrust I felt earlier. I'm just grateful that he's here.

But later, once Faller's gone again and I'm on the phone to Calabretta, I get a shock because he tells me again what he told me yesterday evening – the thing that slipped through the cracks: the old man's worrying again, picking at the same sore spot.

My new office in the public prosecution department is only half as big as my old one. It's more of a storeroom than an office really. The idea was probably to come up with a special cell, just for me, one where only I – and they – know it's a cell. Every time I look out of the narrow window I'm amazed that it isn't barred.

Officially, I have a secretary, but because there's no anteroom to my office, only a corridor, the secretary sits in the outer office belonging to my colleagues in drugs. So obviously she's mainly their secretary and not mine. It doesn't really bother me, if I'm honest. It's just another excuse to crawl out of my cubbyhole. And obviously you don't need a secretary for most things. I'm perfectly capable of phoning the archive myself, for example.

'Morning.'

'Riley here, hello.'

'Yep.'

'I'd like everything relating to Gjergj Malaj, as soon as possible, please.'

'Everything?'

'Everything.'

'From the early nineties to now?'

'Anywhere the name appears.'

'It'll take a while; that's almost a hundred and fifty files.'

'I know,' I say, hanging up.

I open the arrow slit in the wall and light a cigarette.

I hope to smell a faint hint of spring or hear a bird twittering in a tree. But the only thing I notice is the disaster galloping down on us.

*

'Calabretta thinks Faller wants to shaft the Albanian. All by himself.'

I'm standing at the bar at Klatsche's place, a beer in front of me and the boss in person behind the bar.

'Calabretta thinks what?' Klatsche's clattering around, filling the fridge with bottles.

'That Faller's hatched a plan,' I say. 'And that he's about to put his plan into action. He seems to have decided that it's bang out of order to have the Albanian still running around free, especially now he's putting on society airs.'

'It is out of order,' says Klatsche. 'I'm with Faller on that one. That guy's the biggest skunk in town. He ought to be banged up, not going to receptions at the Hotel Atlantic.'

He's stopped putting the bottles away. He's opened a beer and lit a cigarette. There's not much light in the Blue Night; the friendly shimmer in the room mainly comes from the candles on the tables and in golden holders on the red walls. And there's a warm yellow tinge to the blue neon sign above the liquor shelf. It makes no sense. Klatsche insists it's tinged with red, but that's not true. It's yellow. Yet it doesn't turn the blue green. It's nuts.

'Of course he ought to be banged up,' I say.

I'd like to add something clever starting with 'but' to explain why he hasn't been. I can't think of anything. I've been chewing on it for years; we've all been chewing on it for years – decades, it feels like. And Faller won't get the Albanian banged up now. He'll just get himself into trouble. Gjergj Malaj sent him a vicious warning years ago. Faller's suffered for it ever since. Malaj won't warn him off again.

Klatsche knows all this. I don't need to explain it to him. He just watches us as we throw ourselves at windmills and run into brick walls. He's the one who scrapes us out of the corners each time and patches us up with a palette of strong drinks and kind words.

I sigh; we clink bottles.

'You're worried about Faller,' he says.

'He's starting to crack up,' I say. 'He feels too strong. It's not good to feel too strong. You forget to take cover. I mean, we've been through all that…'

'Has he done anything that could be dangerous yet?'

'No idea,' I say. 'According to Calabretta, he hinted that he's planning something soon.'

'Faller was boasting? Doesn't sound like him.'

'He wasn't. Calabretta reckons he's going to need him, and that's why he let him in on it.'

I light a cigarette; Klatsche pushes over an ashtray.

'We've got a top mole on the team then,' he says. 'And I'll keep my ears open in case anyone's noticed any, er, disturbances in the Force, or whatever.' He waves his beer bottle and makes lightsaber noises. 'But he didn't say anything to you?'

I shake my head. 'I met him this morning, and he was just brewing up mysterious stories,' I say. 'Nothing specific. I thought he was feeling good, that's all. Not as crumpled as usual. More like he was having a second spring, if you see what I mean.'

'That all fits,' says Klatsche. 'And if we assume that Faller's not in love, it must be his second spring as a cop.' He draws on his cigarette. 'Fair enough … But the idea of Faller as a lone avenger against organised crime … He's scaring me.'

'Faller or the Albanian?' I ask.

'The combination, sweetheart.' He raises his beer bottle and drinks. 'What's the story with your car, by the way?' he asks.

'Why mention that now?'

He shrugs. 'Talk of fear, maybe.'

'Bollocks, Klatsche. I'm not scared of driving.' I swig my beer. 'The car broke down,' I say. 'I left it in Mecklenburg.'

'And?'

'Garage,' I say, because I don't dare tell him I just left it where it was.

'Garage, uh-huh.' He looks at me.

He knows perfectly well that that's not true.

He says nothing. We drink up our beer. Outside we can hear a police siren on the Reeperbahn.

Then the door opens and a bunch of customers come in. Three women, five men, early thirties, dressed like hipsters. Klatsche's bar is transforming slowly but surely from a red-light dive to a trendy hangout. I bet next year people will come in the mornings and ask if this is a sober rave.

I nip behind the bar, give Klatsche a kiss on the cheek and say, 'Slip me a couple of beers, I've got to go.'

I get the bus to the central station – getting a bus is a bit like going for a stroll. Then I walk down the Lange Reihe; the lights are on now and everyone's out, and I let myself be swept along by all the life around me. This must be what Spiderman feels like when he swings from building to building.

As I walk past the hospital door, the porter greets me almost too cheerfully and I wave back. It's amazing how quickly it happens, how quickly you start to feel like you know each other. The door to room 5 is shut; a policewoman is sitting on the chair, flicking through a magazine. She looks at my pass, we nod to each other, I knock. No reply; I go in anyway.

The man in the bed glares at me. 'You again,' he says hoarsely; I bet it's all he's said all day.

'Yes. Me again. Don't worry, I only came to bring you something.'

Something in his face changes, as if he were entitled to presents in general and he's relieved to see that I've finally grasped that.

I try not to grin and plonk two Astras down on the bedside table. 'Nightcap,' I say.

And I'm gone.

It's rammed in the Blue Night now – there are the hipsters from earlier and a couple of dozen friendly types aged between twenty and fifty, and even a few of the old guard – Ali's regulars, who've never stopped treating the bar like their living room just because

Ali's moved from St Pauli to the Turkish Riviera. Klatsche didn't just take on the furniture and the greasy bar, there was also the entire human stock. He didn't polish or otherwise renovate the noisy ladies and hard-drinking gentlemen though. Their faces have real patina and they've stayed nicely jagged; sometimes you can snag yourself on an awkward corner.

I sit at the far end of the bar, on the last free seat. Actually, it's not even a seat, it's just the draughty corner by the window, which is why no one else is sitting here. I like this corner though. It's close to the alcohol and to Klatsche, and has a good view of the whole pub. And if you really stare, and have a beer or two inside you, you can make out what the Herbertstrasse ladies are saying as they negotiate their fees behind the smeary red glass.

1993, winter.

FALLER, GEORG

He came to Hamburg from Tirana a year or two back. Started small, with gambling. They say he won so much money he was able to buy his first shop outright.

By now, though, he doesn't have to pay much if he wants a shop. Doesn't pay at all, some people say. One of his cousins just has to mention his name. You'd rather give up your shop than your wife's hands or your kids' eyes.

He has huge power. And a very secretive family. There might be sixty of them, or a hundred. We don't know.

We only know that he's declared war on the Kiez.

And on us.

There's an Albanian saying that goes: A wolf licks his own flesh but eats a stranger's.

Sometimes he sends the Italians to do the eating.

They fly in from Palermo or Bari.

Just last week they shot five bullets into the chest of some little adventurer.

He insulted someone. A friend of the Albanian's who's married to a young woman from one of the poshest families in Hamburg.

The Italians got fifty thousand marks for their bloodbath. Plus expenses.

After the murder, they painted the town red.

Or so people say.

MALAJ, GJERGJ

He insulted someone who belongs to me. Someone important. A wise man who married well.

His wife does a lot for me.

I had him slaughtered.

CALABRETTA, VITO

I've got exams.

I've got civilian service to do.

And I've got a German passport now too.

My parents didn't understand.

That I don't want to be an Italian any more.

But I am an Italian anyway. I'll be one forever.

The pizza chef.

Spaghetti.

Parking the bus on the football field.

But I'm a German too. This is my country; I live here. So say hi to English football for me.

I don't know what I'll do after my civilian service. Wait and see what the other Germans do. Uni's not for me, I reckon. Dad would love it if I went. But Dad's hardly ever at home. So I don't need to go to uni for him.

RILEY, CHASTITY

My Dad is dead.

Bullet in the head.

Head on the desk.

I found him.

Since then I've withdrawn from myself.

Or into myself.

Or: a bit of me died with him.

VELOSA, CARLA

I'm pretty. So damn pretty!

Half the harbour's at my feet.

It can be a bit embarrassing sometimes, but basically I'm happy as Larry because everyone's in love with me.

MALUTKI, ROCCO

It was when we were down at the jetties unloading a lorry. You know, 'unloading'. At night.

She cycled past. She was so pretty; I've never seen such a pretty girl. And her scarf blew in the wind as if she had a cloud of butterflies around her neck.

KLASSMAN, HENRI

School.

Kiss my arse.

JOE

There was this woman.

That evening in this hotel bar.

She said I looked lonely.

At that moment I didn't know if I'd rather love her or shoot her. Because her first shot was a bull's-eye.

I ordered her a drink and disappeared up to my room.

The next evening she was there again. She wasn't afraid of me.

I didn't shoot her that time either; I loved her.

I can't let that happen to me again.

WITH THE TIDES IN HIS FEET *OR* AFTER TWO VODKAS THE WORLD FITS A WHOLE LOT BETTER AGAIN

I feel sick; I've eaten too many files. But it was the content, not the number of files, that did it. Not that I didn't know, but swallowing down a hard ball of it all in one go sheds an extra-nasty light on the whole business. And shines a merciless spotlight on our authorities. It's not the fault of the police that the Albanian's had free rein in this city for as long as he wanted, and that he's now sitting pretty in his villa in a classy suburb with a spotlessly clean slate. They did their job to the best of their ability. But in some funny way, it never quite worked out. Search warrants came too late, or not at all. Proceedings were protracted or dropped altogether; witnesses suddenly vanished, or better still, turned up dead.

Of course, I was there – saw all the spanners that were thrown into our works in recent years; but when you're in the middle of it, you can't see the method as clearly as when you look at it from outside, from a little distance. The effect was as if someone had built a protective bubble – invisible to investigators – around the Albanian. As if someone was secretly making sure that nothing could be proved against him that would stand up in court. It can't just have been Chief Prosecutor Schubert, who had more or less drifted into the case. Someone more powerful must have had a hand in it; someone who was much more able to direct the play being staged in our town. People with money and influence and a huge fear of losing both. After a certain point, rich people are no longer driven by their money, but by their fear.

The date on the last file that explicitly mentioned Gjergj Malaj was years ago. It looks as if he'd got right out of everything.

Now he simply manages his empire and clearly has other people to do the work, and to do it so that there's not the slightest connection to him any more.

I can understand it driving Faller crazy, especially after everything that Malaj did to him, but I don't understand why he has a sudden urge to collar him now. I don't understand why he thinks it could work. And I've got no idea what he wants to do.

However, I do understand why he thinks that now he can do it his own way, he might manage things better than when he was on the force. The state could poke its nose into Officer Faller's enquiries, but not a private citizen's. But … if it comes to aggro with the Albanian, a private citizen would be living far more dangerously than a policeman.

Unless he's still got a reliable partner and a loaded gun.

And that's where Calabretta comes in.

I snap the last file shut and put it back in its crate – one of the many stacked around my office since this morning.

It's late afternoon. The soles of my feet are itchy; I want to get out. But there's one more thing to do.

I pick up the telephone receiver and call the Steindamm police station. Ask how enquiries into the Schmilinskystrasse GBH case are going.

They are gathering evidence and searching for witnesses. No concrete leads as yet.

'We have too few staff and too much drug crime, Ms Riley. The half-dead, like your hospital case, are our daily grind. And we have to ensure that we don't get twenty more a week.'

Understood.

Nothing to be done there then.

I thank him and say I'll ring back, but the clerk on the phone and I both know that he probably won't answer.

I hang up, and then Calabretta calls.

'Hey,' I say. 'I've just chewed my way back through every file on the Albanian.'

He doesn't answer. He can't. I can hear that from his breathing. He has no words today. The soft light of yesterday and the day before must have gone out again. Sometimes a wind gusting round the wrong corner is all it takes to blow out a light like that.

'I can be at the Blue Night in two hours,' I say.

He exhales.

'If that's a yes, just hang up, OK?'

Click.

On the way to the hospital, I buy four bottles of beer. I have the impression that idea of mine went down well yesterday. The bottles clatter in my bag, and when I'm suddenly buffeted as my jacket fills with wind on Lombard Bridge, I feel as though those four bottles give me just enough extra weight not to stagger.

His door is open; a rectangle of yellow light falls onto the squeaky grey lino floor in the corridor. I knock on the door frame for formality's sake. The head of his bed is raised; he's sitting motionless, his eyes closed.

But he says: 'Come in.'

'Got a headache?' I ask, pulling a chair up to his bed.

'It's amazing what you can see…' he says. 'Do you happen to have another couple of beers on you?'

'Four,' I say, putting the bottles one by one on the bedside table.

'What else do you do all day, apart from supplying an old cripple with alcohol?'

'I sit in my office at the prosecution service,' I say. 'Well, it used to be an office. Today it's a bloody hole. And you're not a cripple. You're just out of action at the moment. The doctors say it'll all be all right.'

'Why has your office changed? Has someone put up a few walls?' He opens his eyes and looks at me.

'Something like that,' I say, opening two of the beer bottles. 'I pissed a few people off. And made a few other mistakes. Now they hide me in a cupboard.'

I press a bottle into his left hand. Apparently only the lower part of his left arm is broken; the upper arm and shoulder seem to work reasonably well. At least, his arm is splinted in such a way that Mr Austrian Joe can get his hand to his mouth. Perhaps they actually took care to do it that way. So he didn't have to be fed. So he could hold onto his dignity. At least I hope that was one of the reasons they did it that way.

'You're one of the good guys, aren't you?' He looks at me and swigs his beer.

'Sometimes,' I say.

'Sometimes what?'

'Oh. Good guy, bad guy,' I say. 'You can't always say for certain…'

'Oh yes you can,' he says.

We drink and sit in silence. For the whole of the first beer.

It's a bit like drinking with Faller.

On the second beer, I say: 'Now, why don't you just tell me who wanted you in here?'

He looks at me like I'm bad weather. He doesn't like it when I ask questions.

'Why don't you tell me when I'll get a wheelchair so we can go on an excursion down the hallway?'

'Shall I take care of it?' I ask.

'Care is the word.'

He looks at me, his eyes askew. As if he's just been off in another world and has surfed his way back.

Calabretta seems to have been halved over night. There's a concertinaed matchstick man at the bar. His dark hair is hanging blearily over his forehead; the top half of this half-man has tipped face first onto the bar. You couldn't use him for anything, whichever way you held him.

Standing behind Calabretta, by the jukebox, is Klatsche, both thumbs pointing downwards. Standing in front of Calabretta are an empty glass and half a bottle of vodka. Great, well done.

'How long has he been like this?' I ask, pointing at my Italian colleague.

'Weeks,' says Klatsche. 'Haven't you noticed?'

'I meant the head on the bar.'

'He arrived about half an hour ago. He was already fairly well oiled. Then he ordered the bottle of vodka.'

Klatsche reaches for me and pulls me into his arms. He smells of man and freshly mown grass. I could so easily let him eat me up.

'Why give him a bottle of booze?' I ask.

'Because I'm not a monster. Our friend here looked like Betty had sent him an invitation to her wedding.' He lays a hand on Calabretta's head. 'The stupid cow should have ripped out his brain along with his heart, so he wouldn't have to keep missing her. Women are brutal.'

I know that he knows what he's talking about. Klatsche's had plenty of experience of women. My own inner brute is always on the point of breaking out. She's scratched his face a couple of times already. But she shies away from his heart, because she knows that wide-boy hearts have superpowers. If you want to hurt them, with a bit of bad luck you only end up hurting yourself.

Klatsche's hand is still resting on the Calabretta head.

'Shall we bring him back to ours tonight?' he asks.

'Sure,' I say.

He puts two highball glasses on the bar in front of us and fills them with ice, lemon, vodka and tonic, then he stows the vodka bottle back on the shelf. We're about to clink when his phone rings. He says hello; he listens, nods then he says: 'OK, I'm on my way.'

He pushes my drink over to me. 'Can you take over for me till Rocco gets here?'

'Your drink or your bar?'

'Both. Gran's run away. They've rounded her up already, but now she won't stop crying. I've got to go over there.'

I give him a kiss and make my way round behind the bar. I'd better polish the glasses.

'How does your gran keep doing that?'

Klatsche shrugs. 'How would I know? Secret plane. Propeller in her nightie. Or she's got an accomplice.'

I know that he wishes she had one. His parents were drunks and are dead. He didn't have much to do with them. His gran was the only constant in his life. His value system – unshakeable, if not exactly off-the-peg – came from her. Now she's strapped to her bed and can't tell day from night or her grandson from her nurse.

He grabs his leather jacket from the hook and leaves.

He'll spend the night by her bed, hold her hand and tell her stories. When he comes back tomorrow morning, he'll say that she's thinner and more translucent than ever.

He hopes she'll die soon, and he hates himself for hoping that.

I bend over the bar to Calabretta, stroke his hair and say: 'It's shit needing nursing. You get yourself back on your feet, you hear.'

Then I familiarise myself with the situation behind the bar and wonder what actually happens if customers come in. Realisation: I'm mistress of the alcohol, but not mistress of the situation.

But after two vodkas the world seems to fit me a whole lot better again. When a group of young people arrives, I manage to get beer from the fridge without incident and even remember to take money for it. Note: for the first time in what feels like an eternity, I feel really useful for something.

Things run on merrily for a good while. Mostly I sell beer; sometimes I mix a stiff drink. I don't need to worry about the jukebox; right at the start I decide on Screamin' Jay Hawkins on an infinite loop. 'I Put a Spell on You', over and over; a wall of noise in between whiles. Nobody moans, and Calabretta sleeps deeply and peacefully, and I think to myself that we'll get him home and straightened out a bit too. And so, slowly, I start to really enjoy my new job as a barmaid.

Just under two hours later, I'm really in the swing of it, including a corner of a tea towel tucked into my waistband, when the door opens and Carla and Rocco are there. They look tired, but freshly showered and everything, as if they've got plans. Carla's wearing a black roll-neck jumper, skinny jeans, an oversized, dark-grey coat and dizzyingly high heels. Her dark curls gleam radiantly in the candlelight, like her eyes. Rocco's wearing one of his perpetual pinstripe suits, a particularly well-fitting one. He has neither a jacket nor a coat on, just a woollen scarf round his neck and a flat cap on top. His ankle boots are brown and set the tone for the whole outfit. Together, they're stunning: a dark brilliance. You just can't look away when they show up. It was wise of them both to marry each other. They're carved from a single piece of wood.

They come through the room towards me, and it occurs to me again that the most beautiful thing about them, by far the most beautiful human feature of all, is when you can read someone's story in the way they move. Rocco walks like you walk when your dad was a street-corner violinist, when you grew up a hairsbreadth from the kerb yet despite all the hardship there was always a warm bosom to embrace. He walks with the tides in his feet and freedom in his face. Great Freedom – both the best name for a street ever and heartbeat of this city.

Everything about Carla is water and sunset and olive oil and Lisbon.

'Interesting barmaid this evening,' says Rocco, looming in front of me, his hands in his trouser pockets.

'Meaning?' I ask, lighting a cigarette. Time for a well-earned break, I feel.

'Interesting barmaid,' says Rocco with a grin.

Carla has squeezed in next to Calabretta, but it looks more like she's holding him up.

'What's up with *Sorgenboy*?' she asks, stroking his hair.

'Worry Boy's downed half a bottle of vodka and pressed the off switch on his brain,' I say.

'Oh,' she says. 'Has something happened?'

'Nothing in particular,' I say.

Rocco waves it off. 'Part of the process, girls. Classic reset, when a man thinks he's suffered enough. You wait. He'll be much better tomorrow.'

His words settle above our heads like a sermon, and Carla says, 'Right.'

Then we decide that Carla will take over the bar while Rocco and I get Calabretta back to my place.

She takes off her coat, and every eye watches.

It's always an impressive sight.

I hand over my tea towel, Rocco wraps one of Calabretta's arms around his own neck, I take the other, and together we drag our beloved drunk to the exit.

Screamin' Jay Hawkins sings as we go:

'I shot the sheriff but I swear it was in self-defence.'

The moon hangs outside my window; it's waning, and the harbour dust has layered one of its special filters over it. It looks like a large, yellow potato.

I sit on the windowsill. As always when I don't know where to put myself. Lying on my couch is Calabretta; earlier he was waning too, but now he's giving off amazingly strong vibes. He's breathing calmly, he's breathing quietly. He thanked Rocco and me briefly after we'd hauled him up the stairs, then he just lay down, pulled my grey woollen blanket over himself and closed his eyes. It seems to me that he's starting to take care of himself. To sort himself out. It's a bold claim, of course, when he's just drunk himself unconscious, but something's telling me he's on the right path. Perhaps it's just Rocco's diatribe about the self-healing powers of wounded men that he subjected me to in the taxi on the way home.

I tilt the skylight, light a cigarette and look up at the gibbous moon. If I were a wolf, I'd howl. I find myself thinking about Faller, who's always hounded on and on by his hunting instinct. I find myself thinking about the Austrian – about Joe, if that is his name – but nothing much comes to me about him. I find myself thinking about Klatsche's gran and light a candle in my head. Maybe I should pay a visit to the old lady with my victim-protection hat on. I find myself thinking about my dad, who's no longer here; about my mum, who was never there; and about the fact that I never had any proper friends until I had Faller, Calabretta, Klatsche and Carla.

I can't stop staring at the damn moon.

I smoke another three to eight cigarettes, and someone knocks on the door, two long, three short. I stand up and let Klatsche in, and now the moon is no longer the only thing to hold on to around here.

1995, autumn.

FALLER, GEORG

There's a law that applies in every system where people earn a lot of money. It's this: money is earned quietly, we don't make a big deal out of it, and everyone who's in on the earning, kindly shut your gobs.

It's the same for boardrooms, public authorities and mafia families.

It's more than a law for our Hanseatic businesspeople: it's in our DNA – a knowledge, an attitude that people here have had for centuries.

Maybe that's why guys like the Albanian can do better business here than in Naples.

I'm always saying it. I shout it to everyone. But nobody listens. Nobody wants to hear it.

Bollocks, they say. Not on our patch.

Oh man, Faller. Stop that, they say. Never mind about the Albanian.

I ought to stop provoking him. I ought to keep out – out of the Kiez. I ought to shut my mouth and worry about normal dead people.

They can piss right off though. Not the dead – they can't help it. The others. All the ones who don't get it.

Every evening, before I go to sleep, I take aim at him in my mind, at his power and his despotism. Annoy him, disturb his comfort zone, make myself a nuisance to him. Stop him getting past me. And make sure he knows about it.

MALAJ, GJERGJ

He's annoying.

CALABRETTA, VITO

They actually accepted me.

I'm joining the police.

RILEY, CHASTITY

It doesn't matter what I do. It won't bring my dad back.

But he once said: You could be a lawyer.

OK, then. I'll do that. Even if it doesn't help me.

Amazingly, law doesn't bore me. Lawyers do though – they bore me rigid.

VELOSA, CARLA

They want to go back to Lisbon.

I can understand that. But I don't want to go back.

I belong here now. By the harbour. To the gulls.

It's my harbour.

They're my gulls.

What would I do in Lisbon? I don't even speak decent Portuguese any more.

I told my parents to go if they want to. Not to be sad. I'll take over the shop.

KLASSMAN, HENRI

You pocket the comics.

Then you smile.

Then you walk out again.

Then you sell the comics at school for half-price and now everyone wants to buy their comics from you.

It's that easy.

MALUTKI, ROCCO

It works best with rich women from Eppendorf, aged thirty or so. They like to splash the cash. They like a little rascal on their arm.

And if the little rascal gets into a jam and has no idea how it could have happened, they help him.

Of course they never have to do that twice. By then, the little rascal's long gone, he's never coming back.

JOE

I've got a new client.

Can't get his measure. Doesn't matter. In the end, I get everyone's measure.

But we could make something solid of it.

We're equally invisible.

RADIO SCHIZO

Klatsche's still asleep. My colleague Calabretta and I are drinking coffee on the balcony. It's cold but dry, and diving into this icy cold air is good for our heads. At first I thought Calabretta had finally flipped when he said we should drink our coffee outside – when he took my arm and said he always does it, even if it's snowing. Now I think his idea is fabulous. I feel like I'm in pole position for the day. Last night I'd have bet that my first coffee of the morning would only have silently blown my head off, leaving me helplessly roaming the streets in the hope that nobody noticed its absence.

Now I breathe in the cold air and say: 'I'm going round to Faller's. He doesn't like people visiting him at home. It's a neat way to put him off his stride.'

Calabretta looks down to the sleepy street.

'Perhaps I'll find out what he's actually planning.'

Calabretta looks at me. 'And then?'

'What do you mean, "and then"?'

'I'm not at all sure,' he says, 'that what Faller's up to is actually that bad.'

'Well, on the face of it, he's a nice, old grandpa who wants to pick a fight with the biggest predator in town,' I say. 'Of course it's that bad.'

'He's not a nice, old grandpa. He's a cunning old dog. And I've been thinking.'

'When? Yesterday evening with your head on the bar?'

'That's unkind.'

'Sorry.'

Calabretta slurps his coffee and eyes the houses opposite. There's a gang of tradesmen turning cheap flats into expensive ones. Polish the floorboards, replaster the walls, shove in a spa-style shower head, and, wham, seventeen euros a square metre. Excl. bills.

'I don't reckon we could stop him,' says Calabretta, 'whatever he's planning.'

'Maybe,' I say. 'But if we knew a bit more, we could keep a bit more of an eye on him.'

'Or help him,' he says.

I stir my coffee.

Maybe Calabretta has gone mad after all. Sure – let's help Faller take the Albanian down. All on our lonesomes. What a superb idea.

'You're not serious?' I mutter.

He finishes his coffee and stands up. 'Well, I'll be off then. Thanks for taking me in and looking after me so well.'

He stands erect and very straight on my balcony, raises his arms in the air, stretches briefly, and then he's gone.

If I didn't know better, I'd have said he spent yesterday evening weight training.

I finish off my coffee, suck another load of cold air into my lungs and wonder whether to smoke a cigarette or run a lap of the park.

I decide on running. Running time is thinking time.

I don't usually get any results, but it's worth a try.

The good thing about this city is that if you don't feel like getting a bus or a train or a taxi, you can just take the boat. Faller lives close to the Elbe beach, so I get off the ferry at Övelgönne. I watch it sail on for a while because I like the way the old ships tramp over the water. Then I walk the few hundred metres to Faller's house. A white fence, a couple of pruned rose bushes, an apple tree with an old wooden ladder leaning against its trunk. The house is slightly askew – a little beachside idyll. To the left of it is a kind of courtyard. It used to be home to benches and a table; now it's home to the Pontiac. It looks a little wistful here, in this spotlessly swept paradise. As if it were still hoping for this not to be quite the end, please. Hoping that, one day, it will go back to the wide, endless roads on the other side of the Atlantic.

I prefer not to speak to it. I don't want to lie.

Faller comes to the door in slippers, a mug of coffee in his hand.

'Aha,' he says.

'Good morning,' I say.

He looks at me, wrinkles his brow, grimaces, turns away, heads towards the hallway and says: 'Well, you'd better come in.'

I'd love to, thanks: he hates having visitors.

Or maybe he only hates having me visit.

Because it mixes up his two lives: the filthy murder squad life, where he was always having to tackle death and the devil, and where he ended up knocked out, humiliated and shot at; and the nice life where he can climb up a wooden ladder to pick apples. I can understand that. I have two lives too. There's my professional blend of grey and clouds and a wooden feeling in my soul; and then there are the other moments of steaming food at Carla's or a light on still at Klatsche's.

We stand in the kitchen, at the counter under the window. Hanging in front of the window are eggshell-coloured curtains, stopping about halfway down and all flounced and ruffled. It's funny how men always put up with what their wives want.

I don't think Faller's the type to care much about the house. So long as nobody from his other life visits him here.

'Coffee?' he asks, holding up a mug. There's a cat on it.

'Lovely,' I say.

He pours filter coffee into the cat mug; it smells sour – my belly twitches. But I've got to go through with it now.

Faller hands me the mug. I add a little milk and a lot of sugar.

'But you didn't just come round for a coffee,' he says.

'True,' I say, stirring the cat mug. 'I came because I know you're planning something to do with the Albanian.'

He recoils slightly, then says, robotically: 'Also true.'

It's just how I imagined it playing out – knocking him down with it, leaving him so gobsmacked and softened, he'd crumble and be dead easy to crack.

'I'm worried about you,' I say.

He looks at me, serious, honest and without a trace of mockery in his eyes. Takes a sip of the dishwater coffee. Leans his elbows on the worktop so that he can stare through the window under the half-curtains for a round.

After a long five minutes, he says: 'And?'

'And what?'

'What do you want from me?'

'I want you to leave it,' I say. 'It won't get you anywhere. It'll just get you into trouble.'

He carries on staring out of the window.

We drink our coffee in silence and the longer we say nothing, the more it dawns on me that this is a different silence from normal. Normally it feels great to sit in silence with Faller. Now it's like this: instead of not saying anything, we're not talking to each other, and that doesn't feel good at all.

Half an hour later, I give up and pack away my silly idea – the idea that he'd talk to me, that at least he'd want my concern, or at the very least understand it. I shove all those visions back into my badly equipped communication toolbox and make tracks. When there's nothing to be gained, you should stop digging – give up the desperate hope that just maybe you might find a stupid worm after all.

As I leave, I think: I'm watching you, Faller. He stands in the front doorway with a mug of cold coffee in his hand, looking right through me. We don't often part like this.

At the beach, I get on the next ferry back to town.

I stand on deck and breathe in the pictures.

The gulls.

The waves.

The wind.

The dusty light.

The ballet of bustling boats.

The Blohm & Voss shipyard.

There's a rusty ocean giant, only held together by good will.

On the other side are the tourists. They struggle down the jetties in all weathers. They sometimes make it past the souvenir shops, but usually get sucked in by not quite the best fish sandwiches in town. Actually, it's like this: half an hour on the jetties and you start feeling sick. I get out at Bridge Three and head up to the street and take a taxi to St Georg, leaving the tourists to the fish sandwiches and their fate. It's not that I don't want to help. As always, I gave a couple of challenging looks, and as soon as anyone looked back, I said quietly: 'You *can* go to other places, you know.'

But, as always, nobody reacted; they all – mainly the ones with southern German accents – looked at me like I wasn't quite all there.

Some stupid, big-city bitch.

And they're not far wrong.

My taxi driver is a punk. Not just a fashion punkanista but the real deal. Smell and all. You run into one now and again. He asks briefly where I want to go, then turns his music on again. Fierce, a din that blows your ears out. It's quite something.

'What is this?' I yell.

'Radio Schizo!' he yells back. 'Berlin!'

Radio Schizo.

Berlin.

I don't know why, but in a sick kind of way I feel in a very good place with that band name running through my head and the back seat of this taxi under my arse. We dispense with conversation; the roar of Radio Schizo will only tolerate a city rushing past the window, although Bucharest might be more in keeping with the sound than Hamburg.

Four quick songs later, the taxi spits me out again at the Steindamm police station. The punk driver can barely hide his disdain for my destination, but I don't mind that. There's a home port for everyone.

I pull myself together just in time to not accidentally wave after him when he does an illegal U-turn and bombs off towards the railway station.

Inside the police station, a single word flashes at me from every eye I meet: OVERLOAD. It's accompanied by constant questions: Who? Where? What? When? Excuse me? Could somebody just…? Can't you speed it up a bit?

I pause on the threshold for a moment and watch. My colleagues look as though they're trying to lift enormous beams that it's vital to keep up in the air. But the beams aren't all that stable, and there are heavy loads weighing them down: drugs, child prostitution, violence and insanity.

When one of the desk clerks notices that I'm standing there, he looks frantically at me, and then, in despair at the prospect of new jobs to do, asks how he can help me. I say: 'It's fine. I'll come again another time.'

He's already gone, turning his attention to the next ringing telephone. I vanish as if I were a ghost. I'm now certain that I won't make any progress on the Austrian here, whatever his name actually is.

On the way to the same mysterious Austrian, I decide to refine the business with the beer, so I pop into the nearest deli to buy a bit of ham and cheese, and a loaf of bread and a bottle of wine. It's lunchtime after all.

'Does he speak to you?' the policeman outside the hospital room asks, looking ruefully at me. 'For days I've been wishing the man a good morning, or a good afternoon or a good night. And all I get in return is a scowl.'

'Don't take it personally,' I say. 'He only speaks to me when I force him to.' I hold up the bag of grub, the wine bottle peeking out of the top.

'You're bribing him,' the policeman says sternly.

'Wait a minute or two,' I say, 'then you can have some too.'

I slip into the ward kitchen, fetch three plates, three glasses and look for a reasonably sharp knife. The thing I find is a joke. A knife like you used to get in aeroplanes, but don't any more, because somebody actually thinks you could seriously injure someone with one, which is an even bigger joke. Any child in St Pauli has sharper knives. I leave the knife in the drawer. As well as his army pistol, my dad left me a mountain of Swiss Army knives; I always have one on me.

I divvy up the food between the plates: cheese, ham and bread for the Austrian and his guard, cheese and bread for me. Red wine for everyone, even though two of us are on duty. When I present the officer in the hallway with his set menu, he gives me a brief look of surprise. I look wryly back at him, and with that the matter is settled.

'OK, then,' he says.

'Enjoy,' I say.

Instead of 'Hello' or 'Thank you for the delicious food and good company', the Austrian says: 'There's no need.'

'Are you that keen on hospital slop?'

'I mean your colleague outside,' he says.

'It's for me to decide whether he's necessary or not.'

'No one will do anything to me,' he says.

'Looking at you,' I say, 'I beg to differ.'

He puts his head slightly to one side, as far as he can in his current plastered condition. 'I mean, nobody will kill me.'

'Why are you so sure of that?' I ask.

'I've got life insurance,' he says, and with his Austrian lilt it sounds almost like he's said 'honoured to make your acquaintance'.

I put a slice of ham on some bread for him and press it into his left, unbandaged, hand.

'Do you have what they call "life insurance" in the Kiez,' I ask, 'or a piece of paper with the name of a big company at the top?'

He bites into his bread and chews. He seems to be enjoying it.

'Something in between,' he says; chews, swallows. 'Could I have some of the cheese please?' He opens his mouth.

Somewhat taken aback, I nod and pop a bit of cheese between his teeth.

'"Something in between"? What's that supposed to mean?'

'That,' he says, chewing, 'can mean whatever you want it to. Aren't you eating? And what about the wine?'

'Tell me what you mean about the life insurance,' I say, 'and I'll give you a glass.'

He looks out of the window for a while. A tiny bit of the sun is about to break through the clouds.

'I've got a bank box in Switzerland,' he says. 'If I die, sooner or later people like you will come and have the box opened. There are a couple of other people who know that I've got the bank box, you see – and it is not in their interests for that to happen.'

I don't believe it. A bank box full of great, big secrets. And I don't even know the man's real name.

'Which other people?' I ask.

He screws up his forehead, twists his mouth, shakes his head a fraction and says: 'Mh.'

I've only seen this way of not talking about things from Calabretta. And certain gentlemen in the vice squad. I make a note of it and hand him the glass, half full of red wine. As I do so, I notice his right hand, which seems to have been freshly bandaged.

'How's your hand?' I ask.

'How should it be? There used to be five fingers and now there are only four.'

'Why did they do that?' I ask.

A grin plays around the corners of his mouth. 'Because they didn't know I'm left-handed.'

'Who didn't know?' I ask, sliding a little closer to his bed. 'Come on, spit it out. Who are you talking about?'

'Have you got a cigarette?' he asks.

'You're not allowed to smoke in here,' I say with growing impatience and point at the bandage. 'Joe, who did this?'

He empties his glass and holds it out to me. I refill it.

'Thanks,' he says, downing it again. In one. The whole glass.

I can guess what's going to happen in the next second, and it does: drinking red wine so fast, on top of the painkillers – it's like liquid tar on his eyelids. I can actually see them getting heavier.

'You're one of the good guys,' he says. 'Like I said, just believe me.'

I put my hand on his arm. 'Joe,' I say.

He's not really trying to keep his eyes open, but I think he's listening.

'Who did you mess with?'

'I underestimated them,' he says quietly. 'I thought I was too big for them.' He yawns. 'But they have no respect.' He yawns again. He yawns like he wants to eat me. 'That's very bad.'

I scent the chance to catch hold of his subconscious and maybe get some information.

'What's your name, Joe? What's your real name? Tell me who you are, please.'

His eyes are shut.

'I were a good boy,' he whispers. 'I were a very good boy.'

Then he falls asleep.

He breathes slowly and deeply, and great peace spreads over his face.

Who could have known the guy drinks red wine like apple juice?

I refill my own glass, take a piece of bread and a lump of cheese and chew away in frustration.

Then something occurs to me.

Going out of the door, I'm glad to see my colleague on the hard chair is enjoying his lunch. I look for the nurses' station and, because no one's there, I simply call down the corridor:

'Could I speak to a doctor for a moment, please?'

2002, spring.

FALLER, GEORG

He won't get rid of me.

HE.

WON'T.

GET.

RID.

OF.

ME.

And there's something not quite right about this prosecutor.

MALAJ, GJERGJ

There he sits. Mr Public Prosecutor. In front of an expensive glass of wine.

His pale suit has dark stains under the arms.

The guy is made of fear and arrogance. I swear he'll lick my balls yet.

RILEY, CHASTITY

Going to Hamburg soon. Got a job in the public prosecution service.

I don't think I'll stay long. I really want to get to Berlin.

CALABRETTA, VITO

Murder squad, four weeks now.

All OK there.

And I like my boss.

He's snappish as an old watchdog.

KLASSMAN, HENRI

That was a dead cert, a sure thing. Copier out of the lobby and into the car and out of the car again to the fence.

No partner. No one to talk. Nothing to go wrong.

For the life of me, I've no idea who grassed me up.

Now I'm sitting here with this weirdo cellmate. Hey ho. I'll stick out a couple of months. Jail doesn't break you that fast.

I'll be fine. I hope.

MALUTKI, ROCCO

I know him by reputation. I thought he wanted to be the next burglar king. He thought so too. Seems it didn't quite work out.

I give him half my bread every evening. The kid's always starving; must be still growing.

I don't like this ugly rye bread you get here. And there's no one to bring you a decent white loaf. Or a slice of cake.

That's all.

VELOSA, CARLA

My first slice of cake.

My first latte.

My first customer.

Six months renovating. Alone. The works.

Now there are old chandeliers hanging wonkily from the ceiling. That means the walls aren't straight either, but they glitter so prettily.

I spend the whole day taking photos of the first day.

JOE

The longer I do this job, the more I disappear. Sometimes I don't even know myself if I'm actually still there.

Fine by me.

I'D LIKE TO GO SOMEWHERE, RIGHT NOW, WHERE I CAN SMOKE

It rains and squalls, and then the sun shines again. The sky's in motion, spring's showing its forceful side. On the radio they say there's a storm coming in this afternoon. I'm standing in my kitchen, a glass coffee mug in my hand; the clouds outside my window are racing eastwards. It's just beautiful. When the weather's all turned inside out. The hair stands up on the back of my neck and I get an age-old feeling in my belly. Like there's a fight ahead. Like something's really about to go off.

But it's usually wrong.

It usually is really only the weather.

I go for a shower, get dressed and walk to my office. See if there's anything on.

Of course there's nothing on.

I don't exist in the department any more. I'm as invisible here as I was yesterday at Steindamm police station, but there's a subtle yet toxic difference. Here, it's deliberate. As if there was a new regulation: wherever possible ignore Riley, so that one day she'll simply dissolve into thin air all by herself.

Nothing being on doesn't take long, and now it's raining like the angels have knocked over their bucket, so I take a taxi to St Georg.

The wheelchair is standing outside the hospital room, as discussed. I really had to work hard on the young doctor yesterday to get it. At first he acted like he didn't want his patient to leave his bed, but then he blurted out the real issue:

'Who's paying for all this?'

'We'll talk about that tomorrow,' I said, and we will. The child doctor and me.

Today he looks a little older than yesterday; he doesn't look seventeen any more: he looks more like nineteen, or maybe twenty. He looks like he's just off a hard night shift and he knows there's another night shift ahead, and he won't get home before tomorrow morning. And that's probably precisely the case. He's standing next to the wheelchair, holding the thing with his right hand gripping the backrest. As if to say, 'This is my wheelchair'.

'We still have no idea who the man is,' he says. 'We have no personal data, no insurance information, nothing. Social security will pay if he's homeless. But this man arrived in a fancy suit and won't tell us his name. We won't get anything out of them, I can tell you that much.'

'What does he say about it?' I ask the infant doctor, and fall deeper than I was really intending into his tired eyes.

'He said he'd pay cash. I said that he'd have racked up quite a bit on the meter by the end. He said, "That's fine".' He shakes his head ever so slightly. 'The guy's a puzzle to me.'

'Me too,' I say.

He smiles at me.

OK.

I smile back.

He lets go of the wheelchair, slips his hands into the pocket of his demigod coat, inhales deeply and breathes out again.

'Have a good trip,' he says, and then: 'See you.'

Er, yeah.

Carting someone from a bed to a wheelchair when nearly all his bones are broken is almost impossible. Especially when the patient to be carted is tall and imposing, and understandably mostly concerned with preventing his hospital gown, tied on only with two strings at the back, from slipping off. I can understand that. Those gowns are degrading enough when you're lying still. When you're moving, they're just plain mean. So I shove and pull and push carefully – but with all my strength – at the gentleman held together by splints; my neck muscles hang out the stop signs and I get the feeling I'll need a few splints myself in a moment, or at least some drugs. It's only when I tell him there are cigarettes waiting if he gets into the chair that he gives his body a decent shake at the hips, and all at once there he is, actually sitting in the thing. Legs propped up, arms out at an angle.

Lying down, there was something pious about his posture; now he looks more like a big cartoon character who's been bashed about by an even bigger cartoon character. He looks as though someone has grabbed him and hurled him against a wall with all their strength.

But what I say is: 'Looking good.'

He gives me a tormented glance. 'I'd like to go somewhere, right now, where I can smoke.'

'I know,' I say and pull his blanket off the bed, laying it over his legs.

He growls.

I say: 'It's cold out.'

We head off. In front of me is the back of his big head, his short, silvery hair, all kinked from lying down, his powerful neck, his constantly surprisingly broad shoulders. I sense that he's tense, that he feels watched – by everyone and everything. I notice that he's in exactly the same state as I've been in every time I've found myself at police HQ since I became a kind of outsider – the state of having slipped out of the world.

I wonder if even he actually knows exactly which world is his.

In the old days, hospitals still had smoking cages – those glass boxes like you get at airports. Generally a shabby waiting room with the window open, whatever the temperature. After all, if people smoke, they're not going to have anything wrong with their lungs, are they? Or at least, not yet.

Of course there's nothing like that in hospitals any more. If you want to fuck yourself up, you have to put a bit of effort into it. Or at least stand outside, right in the wind.

We take the lift down. I stand next to his wheelchair; we don't look at each other. I stare at the ceiling; he looks straight ahead.

Down at the bottom, I weave him quickly left then right. I wish it was Klatsche in the wheelchair, or Carla, or some other Ernie type, so I could be Bert and we could have some fun.

No idea if Joe notices me using his wheelchair for rally driving. I don't know how Austrians think about that stuff. He ought to appreciate it, because of Niki Lauda. He says nothing.

Outside the door, I park him by a bench. It's pretty windy, but the sun's just shining now; it'll be all right for a couple of fags. I pull a cigarette from my coat pocket, light it and stick it in his mouth.

He goes at it like he went at the red wine yesterday evening. He does things the way someone does the things they always do alone. Without caring about incidental noises. If nobody's ever there to do the normal stuff with you, you just march more ruthlessly through whatever you do. He smokes like an efficient machine. I look at him and suddenly it all becomes clear: I'm the first regular company he's had for years. Probably the first for decades. And it's because he can't run away.

When he's finished smoking, he looks at me.

'Thanks,' he says.

'What for?'

'For being a good guy,' he says, pulling up the right-hand corner of his mouth.

'Stop that,' I say. 'I want to get something out of you, that's all.'

'I know.'

'And?' I ask. 'Am I in with a chance?'

He looks at me.

One minute.

Two minutes.

Three minutes.

Roughly.

I light another cigarette and give it to him. Then one for me. We look each other in the eye again.

We smoke.

After a few deep drags, there's nothing left of his cigarette but ash and smoke and a crushed filter. He chucks it away and says: 'I need to think. Come again tomorrow evening.' And after a brief pause he says: 'Please.'

Course I'll come again tomorrow evening. I've got nothing else on.

I wonder if he knows that.

Rocco's cooked for everyone. The café door is shut and there's a sign in the window saying 'closed'. But people still knock. It looks so lovely in here. It's warm, almost humid, we have no jackets on, and red cheeks. Outside, Hamburg's caught in a storm. It's been pouring since late afternoon; the fire brigade keeps getting called out to pump out the cellars near the Elbe. Now it's gradually calming down, it's only drizzling puppies and kittens now, but the city's not exactly at its most welcoming. I can understand people wanting to come and join us. But sadly I can't help them there.

We've pushed a few of the small tables together; we're sitting by five big plates, Carla, Rocco, Calabretta, Faller and me. There's a tin waiting for Klatsche in the kitchen; we'll fill it later and take it round to him. In the middle of the table there's an Indonesian salad with loads of vegetables bathed in a thick peanut sauce. And two grilled octopuses, crisp outside, tender inside, the colour of rust. We drink rosé from thick glasses.

We don't talk much. Carla and Rocco have talked and yelled and shouted enough today, and Faller, Calabretta and I aren't generally what you might call chatterboxes.

We're eating.

We're together.

It warms our hearts as well as our bellies.

Rocco and Carla call it mixing the glue. Holding the family together. We do this every few weeks. And every few weeks, something's different. A different person needs a bit more glue than the rest. For months, it was me. Then it was Calabretta. Today, nobody really knows. Calabretta's turned in on himself, but seems stable and fairly solid, staring out at the world as if he were a sphinx. Faller looks a bit like his Pontiac. Not pale blue, but a glittering sort of silvery grey, with a face out of late-sixties America. And when he does say something, it's the same rumble.

There's schnapps for dessert.

After two glasses, Faller stands up, picks up his hat and coat. 'I'll be off then.'

We stare.

'Where to?' I ask.

He shakes his head and just rumbles: 'Got to go out again.'

'OK then,' says Carla, going to the door and opening it.

She hugs Faller and comes back to the table. Rocco starts clearing up.

Outside we can hear a dark spluttering. Faller's starting the Pontiac.

'Something wrong?' Carla asks when she sees my face.

'Maybe I should go after Faller,' I say.

She looks blankly at me. She has no idea.

'I thought we'd take Klatsche something to eat and stretch the evening out at the Blue Night,' she says, and then, to Calabretta: 'Should she go after Faller?'

'No,' says the Sphinx. 'She shouldn't. If anyone should go after Faller, it should be me.'

Carla shrugs. 'Suit yourselves,' she says. 'I'll go to the kitchen and pack up the food for Klatsche. You've got that long to figure out if you're coming with us.'

She grabs the rest of the plates and shoves the chair hard enough with her hip it crashes – gently – into the table. She always does that when her mood's tipping from busy towards I'm-not-sure-I-can-take-any-more.

I try to avoid Calabretta's Egyptian stare and ask: 'Smoke?'

He nods and before I can reach for my coat, he's got it in his hand and is laying it across my shoulders. He holds the door for me; I offer him a cigarette. Calabretta only smokes when I smoke.

I give him a light.

'So what's he doing now?' I ask. 'He's not heading home to watch the NDR *Talk Show*.'

'I don't know what he's doing,' says Calabretta. 'But it's none of our business, is it? Or he'd tell us about it.'

'That's how you see it?'

'That's how I see it,' he says. 'A man's gotta do what a man's gotta do.'

'James Stewart?'

'Gary Cooper.'

He reaches out his hand and catches a couple of rain ribbons. His dark eyes gleam. Very slowly, life is reawakening within him.

'Aren't you at all worried about Faller?' I ask.

'Is there anyone who doesn't need worrying about?'

I think. Nobody comes to mind.

'Let's not deceive ourselves,' he says, chucking away his cigarette. 'The times when you could save anyone from anything are over. Good night.'

'Where are you going?'

'Home,' he says. 'I'm going to try and spend a night at my flat for a change.'

'And if you can't?'

'I'll ring you,' he says. 'Say goodbye to Carla and Rocco for me.'

He briefly lays his hand on my shoulder, then he does up his leather jacket and vanishes towards Altona. I watch him go, until he's swallowed up by the drizzly haze. His boots make cowboy noises on the wet cobbles.

I smoke another cigarette and feel abandoned by Calabretta. The way you always feel when someone you've spent a while caring for is getting back on their feet. And, hey, it was him who put the bee about Faller and his Albanian hunt in my bonnet. Now he's acting like it's nothing.

Thanks for that.

Carla's café windows are almost completely misted over; I can just about see in through the clear space left in the middle. Carla and Rocco are behind the bar, standing opposite each other and talking. I can't hear what they're saying but I can see that it's a serious conversation. Carla's shaking her head. Rocco's gesticulating. They're not getting anywhere; Carla's started gesticulating now too – she throws her hands up in the air, the cloth that she was presumably about to wipe a table with almost landing in Rocco's face. They're both talking louder now, but I only hear fragments. And then Carla suddenly turns round. Turns her back on Rocco. Lifts up her hair and holds the bare nape of her neck towards him. The tension ebbs out of his body. He pushes a hand into the dark curls. They stand like that for a long second or two. Then he pulls her to him with his free hand and lays his mouth on her neck. It looks a bit like he's biting her, but their little dance is too tender for that. I've smoked my cigarette to the end but daren't go back in.

Whatever they're doing, it's very private.

They pull away from each other. Carla turns around, kisses her husband on the lips and goes to wipe the table. Rocco disappears into the kitchen. I hold my breath for a moment, then, slowly and noisily, I open the door and walk back in.

'Calabretta sends his regards,' I say. It's meant to sound casual. I don't think it succeeded.

'Has he gone?' asks Carla. There's a strange expression in her eyes. her cheeks are slightly flushed. She looks as though she and Rocco have just had sex.

'Yeah, he's gone home,' I say.

'Well, how about that?' she says. 'Are we cool with it?'

'I think it's OK,' I say.

'Then it's OK,' she says, smiling at me. She goes to the bar, picks up a brown-paper bag and presses it into my hand.

'Here,' she says. 'Can you take Klatsche something to eat?'

'Aren't you two coming too?' I ask.

'Er…' She ums and ahs a bit.

I see. They've got plans.

'I see,' I say.

'Thanks,' she whispers. 'And now, clear off.'

'Thanks for this evening,' I say, but she's already vanished into the kitchen.

I turn the light off, go out and pull the door to behind me.

It's stopped raining. The clouds suddenly break up. You can even see a few stars in the sky.

I turn up my coat collar, light a cigarette and get on my way.

People are bunched outside the door at the Blue Night, and they're standing *in* the doorway too, so it looks like they're spilling out. The joint is boiling over. Inside it's all Motown classics – Klatsche's weekend music.

I say 'excuse me' and 'sorry' and 'could I just?' and work my way through the door and bit by bit over to the bar. Klatsche's brown shirt is open, the white vest he's wearing underneath is clinging to his chest and his dark blonde hair is wet, but because it's so thick and so all over the place, it's still sticking up from his head. He's sweating and toiling, and he's smiling at me. He's so busy with glasses and bottles it's like he's got eight arms.

'Hey, Mr Octopus,' I say.

'Hey,' he says from the other side of the bar.

I hold up the paper bag.

'Food!' he cries

'Do you want it?' I ask.

He nods, reaches an arm across the bar, takes the bag from me and puts it behind him on the shelf below all the liquor bottles.

'Where is everyone?' he asks.

'Oh, them,' I say. 'They had other plans.'

'My girl's here, that's the main thing,' he says, leaning over the bar again; he reaches for my head with his long arms, pulls me to him and gives me a sweaty kiss.

Then he piles on the pathos: 'Could you help me out a bit, please?'

I squeeze past people, which works out OK because everyone's moving to the music, and they're actually all on the same beat. Behind the bar, I take care of the bottles – beer, cola, lemonade and water – while Klatsche deals with all the drinks in glasses. He's mainly mixing long drinks. It's still early, a long way off midnight. So the twenty-schnapps orders aren't due for another couple of hours or so.

We dispense drinks, making it a party. One day, I'll pack in the whole bureaucratic lark and open a pub. I'll call it The Last Cigarette.

'I've got to pop downstairs,' says Klatsche, opening the hatch to the cellar. 'Out of gin.'

I hand four beers over the bar to a woman in a grey coat and cash ten euros.

Before I can take the next order, I hear Klatsche yell from the cellar: 'Come down a mo, babe!'

I climb down through the hatch. It's cool and damp and dark – I can hardly see. There's only a fragment of the dim light prevailing upstairs. And only half the racket makes it down here too.

'Klatsche?'

'Over here.'

He's standing right at the back on the left, in the darkest corner.

'What are you doing there?' I ask, but instead of answering, he takes two steps forward and pulls me to him in the corner. He presses me against the wall and sticks himself to me. At my back is the cold stone, in front is his warm, charged body, sizzling under the beads of sweat. His eyes gleam as dark green as Loch Ness. I remember standing there once, years ago; he took my hand by the deep, cold loch and said: 'Imagine if this were forever.'

It gave me a shock and I pulled my hand away.

In the evening, it cost us a bit in beer and whisky until we were OK again.

He presses me harder against the wall. He thrusts one hand under my T-shirt and undoes first my belt buckle and then his; he does all this very quickly and skilfully, and there's a weight behind it, an urgency – there's no way, absolutely no way at all, of resisting it, and he keeps on, and then he lifts me up a bit, and I say 'Oops', and for a second I think: seriously, now? Against the wall? And then there's no more thinking and I hear the people up above calling for beer and Klatsche hears them too, but we don't care.

We're back up there again before they can leave.

Later on, when it's almost morning and all the customers have gone, we go back down to the cellar again. Because it feels like that's our hot new place – a place that suits us better than anywhere else. And before we go home, Klatsche takes a thick, black felt-tip and draws a bed on the damp wall.

'So it's more comfy for you next time,' he says, although he knows I'm not much into cosiness.

When we turn down our street, the sky's just turning pink and the first birds are twittering their crazy songs.

Just for the record: this is a highly unusual night and unusual nights are always giving notice of something.

2003, summer.

FALLER, GEORG

They say he wants to take a back seat. Get out of business operations.

I can imagine why. He'd rather sit in his comfortable villa on the Elbe and let his army of gangsters do the work. The main job being to spread fear and terror through the Kiez. Stop anyone from thinking this'd be a good time to start anything.

As for his other important job – his property businesses in the Hafencity – he's got the city Senate to do that for him.

You just have to keep shaking the right hands and tormenting the right souls.

Everyone knows, but shush.

Don't talk about it.

It could be bad for business. It could screw up the money.

That's the general plan, and his particular plan too.

But I'm going to take you down, you arseholes.

Sweated through three shirts today.

MALAJ, GJERGJ

Five cousins from Tirana. Boys, hungry guys.

I said they can show me their moves for a while. Do a few things for me. Whoever does best can try for my legacy. I've had it up to here with scummy nightclubs. I'm getting into the better clubs now.

They've sorted out the public prosecutor. It was all getting too obvious with him. But a new one's on order.

And a new pool.

CALABRETTO, VITO

I'm the chief's right-hand man.

The other two are fine with that. They act as his legs and do a lot of running around outside. It suits them down to the ground. They're both the more outdoors type anyway.

Meanwhile the chief and I do a lot of sitting in the office and talking about the Albanian and the structure he's built up. We're looking for holes in it. Places to stick in our fingers and winkle out information. Perhaps we'll even make a few holes in it ourselves.

We investigate with sharpened pencils behind our ears and our minds racing.

I think the boss sees me as the Neapolitan Camorra specialist. Hmm. OK, so I spend my summers with my family near Vesuvius, but I really don't have much to do with the Camorra.

I once mentioned in passing that my uncle was killed doing anti-mafia work. Perhaps it made too much of an impression on the chief.

I barely knew my uncle. But I always thought his *carabinieri* uniform looked ultra-smart in most of the photos. And I liked the fact that his patrol car was an Alfa. A dark blue 165. All *carabinieri* drive Alfa Romeos. There's one outside every barracks, ready to roll. When you're a *carabiniere*, you just jump in and drive off, blue lights flashing, to drink your coffee. Otherwise they don't get themselves worked up over much. Or that's always my impression.

But when I watch my boss with the Albanian business eating away at him, it worries me a bit.

I don't know if he's still got enough distance from it. Maybe he should be a bit more of a coffee-*carabiniere*.

Sat in the office in a vest and shades today.

RILEY, CHASTITY

Nobody wanted the job.

Red-light district, organised crime.

Too much politics, my colleagues said. But you'll be fine, Ms Riley.

My predecessor was an impenetrable guy. My colleagues say that too. 'Cos of all the politics, they reckon. You don't want to go round being too transparent, or it'll come back to bite you.

Dunno what they mean. I'll keep well out of it. I've always kept out of that kind of stuff. Politics and criminal prosecution are two different kettles of fish.

If you mix them, the end result will taste weird.

It just sounded interesting, especially after all the pretty criminality. So I waved my straight As around. You can always leave. And I live in St Pauli, don't I?

That works, said the attorney general. Schubert, that creep.

Whatever. So long as I don't have to sit on his lap.

I'm glad about Faller. He's a bit like my dad. A Robert Mitchum type.

I have to be careful that I don't just lay myself down by him one day. Head on his shoulder. Daddy. But he always looks so kindly at me.

We'll be working together a lot from now on, he says.

Why, I asked, are you organised crime as well as the murder squad?

So he tapped his hat, turned and said: You know.

Oh, right, yeah. So I've heard. There must be overlaps.

There was a time when the Albanian mafia were bumping people off almost like a production line. And then it did get political; even I heard about that.

Well, I'll see; find the most sensible way to keep out of it.

Talking of keeping out – last week, I got a new neighbour. Very young. Bristly dark-blonde hair. Green eyes, freckles. Over six foot tall. Kind of a cross between a skater and a small-time gangster. Wears a rank leather jacket and oversized self-confidence.

On the stairs yesterday, I felt like he was staring at my arse. I didn't know what to do.

I mean, that's not my style – flirting on the stairs etc. And I'm at least ten years older than him.

It's insanely hot again today, everyone's going round in unbuttoned shirts and tiny, thin dresses. I'm wearing jeans and a T-shirt and boots.

I'm not making a spectacle of myself.

KLASSMAN, HENRI

New gaff.

Plus new neighbour. Classy girl. But dressed like she was on an expedition to the North Pole.

Maybe someone could give her a bikini.

Well, now. I don't have time for women. Got to look after my new business. I'm a businessman now. Yessir.

St Pauli Key Service. Quick, cheap and friendly. Open twenty-four seven!

With your experience of locked doors, says Rocco, you'll eat them for breakfast.

I'm going for a beer, barefoot.

MALUTKI, ROCCO

I live in a little hut by the beach and I'm building a boat.

I'm learning on the job. Mirko's teaching me. I always wanted to learn. When the boat's ready, I get my pay. Then we build the next boat.

But before that we go out on the lash, says Mirko, in Dubrovnik.

We drive over in the morning, drink all day and all night, and dance with the prettiest girls, and the next day we drive back to our beach.

Our beach is pebbly. The water glitters turquoise and there are diamonds dancing on the tiny waves. It's so hot and the air is so soft. This is the Caribbean, not Croatia, I tell Mirko every day, and he laughs and says: Perhaps.

He used to have a restaurant in St Pauli. His parents went to

Hamburg before the Iron Curtain closed. After the war in Yugoslavia, Mirko went back to Croatia, where he'd never been till that day.

My home, he says, looking at the mountains behind the coastline.

One evening, when we were sitting by the water with a couple of bottles of beer and a barbecue and two steaks, he asked me where my home was.

Hmm, I said. St Pauli, maybe. Or maybe South America. Or Poland.

South America? Mirko asked.

Someone in my mother's family is from there.

Poland?

My father was a Pole.

Oh, Mirko said.

My mother, I said, always told me I had gypsy blood.

Then you're in the right place with me, Mirko said, licking his knife.

In the mornings, when I can get up and do, or not do, whatever I like, when I could go where I want; in the mornings when I have the strongest sense of not being banged up, that's when I find myself thinking about Klatsche.

I wonder whether his key business is working out. Whether he's got a girl.

Guys like him always have a girl.

Klatsche Klassman and I were released at almost the same time. I picked him up when he got out.

He took me to the station when I left for Croatia.

We slapped each other on the shoulders and laughed. Now I miss him. Funny – in jail you usually make enemies, not friends.

Oh boy, oh boy, oh boy, it's hot here.

VELOSA, CARLA

A scorching summer.

It's been hot and dry for weeks now. At night you can see Mars gleaming. It shines more darkly than all the other stars in the sky.

It's not a star, say the clever dicks, it's a planet.

I don't care.

I met someone, at a fish stall in Övelgönne.

An odd woman. She's got a funny name, something American, hard to remember. Her hair's American too, so glossy and thick and shiny; her hair belongs in a TV series. She can drink like a man. And she's a public prosecutor.

Not at all what I was expecting.

We laughed so much. When a big ship went past, followed by a big wave, the harbour water caught us. Everyone at the stall was soaked through. And I was feeling so silly that I stuck a herring in my mouth. Sideways. She was great.

She's planning to pop into my café at the weekend. Then I'll make her the best coffee in the world and then she won't be able to stop popping in.

JOE

Three at a stroke, and they didn't notice till the last second that they were for it.

That matters to me.

I don't want them to suffer for long.

Hunter's honour.

ESPERANTO

No idea how we made it home. It's pretty impressive that we made it at all in our twisted condition. I wake up briefly when Klatsche gets up around noon to go shopping, but fall asleep again immediately. He's always the one who goes shopping. He lugs food home, he fills his fridge, and he always brings me back the things I need – milk, coffee, vodka and a few apples and bananas.

He looks after me and now I can actually bear to let him.

When I finally wake up, because Klatsche's come home from shopping, it's half past three. That took him a while.

He puts the paper bag of my things on the landing and drags the rest of the bags into the kitchen, where he divides his booty between his caves – fridge, larder, kitchen table. I keep my eyes shut and listen to the racket. Family sounds, I think, and don't know what to make of that.

I open my eyes, look into the sky and see a tentative March sun. I turn over; my shoulder blades hurt. I remember the wall from last night again, and I'm almost a bit embarrassed. Klatsche and I have known each other for years, and for years we've been sometimes more and sometimes less a couple, more often more these days. But when we stood against that cold wall in the cellar yesterday it was like a stormy encounter between two strangers. Lights that had accidentally collided and become entangled in each other. A hasty miniature firework.

I try to stretch my shoulders. It hurts. I shut my eyes again.

Klatsche's making coffee. It clatters and then starts bubbling. Between me closing and opening my eyes, he's sitting next to me on the bed, holding out a mug.

'Hot stuff, baby,' he whispers.

I've stopped bothering to tell him not to call me 'baby'. He won't stop anyway. He always says he'll stop when I stop all the other stuff. And I don't want to think about 'all the other stuff', so I scoot up a bit, take the coffee from him and say, 'Thanks.'

He looks at me as if it's the first time I've woken up in his bed, as if we've only met yesterday, and it's actually a bit like that. He looks at me like that for quite a while. I like it.

I drink coffee and look back at him.

Then it seems like he's looked enough and he switches mode.

'I spoke to a few people,' he says, 'about Faller.'

'When?' I ask, sitting upright.

'Just now,' he says. 'I went back to the Blue Night because I wanted to check that we locked up properly this morning. And I bumped into some guys.'

'And what do those guys say?'

'They're all wondering why old Faller is suddenly prowling round the Kiez so ferociously.'

'What d'you mean, prowling *ferociously* round the Kiez?'

'Well,' says Klatsche, 'he seems to be in a different joint every evening. Always drives up in style in his Pontiac, drinks two beers and drives off again.'

'That's it?' I ask.

'No,' says Klatsche with a frown. 'He tells stories.'

'What kind of stories?' I ask, instinctively knowing they won't be funny ones.

'He talks about the Albanian,' says Klatsche. 'He tells anyone he can get his hands on about everything Gjergj Malaj's done in the last twenty, thirty years. He really does tell them everything.'

'No,' I say.

'Yes,' says Klatsche. 'He talks and talks and talks. Every evening.'

'What does that mean then?'

Klatsche raises his eyebrows. 'Pure provocation,' he says. 'Beats me what he thinks it'll achieve.'

'Perhaps he wants to break through the Albanian's reserve,' I say. 'Make him react to his blathering … so he slips up…'

'But he can't really think that'll work, can he?'

'It's the only explanation I can think of.'

'The most the Albanian will do is set one of his guard dogs on him,' says Klatsche. He takes a gulp of his coffee. 'And to be honest, that's not so unlikely.'

'To be honest,' I say, 'it's highly likely. Malaj's officially – and very skilfully – pulled himself out of everything these days, and gets invited to the very best parties. He's not exactly going to let himself be screwed over by the cop he went to all that effort to get rid of, back in the day.'

'So who's going to get the old boy to drop the bullshit now?'

Klatsche stares out of the window as if the answer to his question might just fly past.

'I'll try,' I say. 'Can you find out where he's already been?'

'I can,' says Klatsche. 'And I can light a candle for him now, to be on the safe side.'

Let's hope candles are like umbrellas – if you've got one, you won't need it. If you haven't got one, you'll get soaked.

The Austrian holds his face into the last remnants of spring sunshine. The wind's moved on. The sun isn't really warming, but it's nice to know it's there. It's a first glimpse of what it'll be capable of in six or seven weeks' time.

He looks pale. Hair and face almost seamlessly grey. Everyone's pale at this time of year, and the effort of clinging onto a hard wheelchair when you're so broken makes you a notch or two paler. This man, who acts like he's made of granite, has a whole lot of cracks.

But smoking seems to help a bit. I'm not so bad with a fag in my mouth, Doctor.

We've been here in our smokers' corner for a good half-hour. He was already sitting in the wheelchair when I arrived at his room.

He didn't exactly look like he was waiting for me, but it wasn't far off.

And now it doesn't exactly look like he's bursting to tell me something – but that's not far off either. His face is turned more towards the sun than to me – I can only see his profile – but for the first time I sense that he might really be prepared to talk to me.

'Go on,' I say. 'Spill the beans.'

He opens his eyes a little, but keeps his face in the sunlight. 'Hmm.'

'Hmm?'

'Mh.'

'I'm not letting up,' I say. 'If you want me to stop pestering you, you need to tell me who beat you to a pulp.'

'Well, listen up then,' he says.

'I'm listening.'

'Really?'

'Really.'

'It won't take long.'

'I believe you.'

He says: 'OK.'

He breathes deeply in and out again. Smoke into the lungs and smoke out of the lungs.

'It's to do with drugs. The bad shit. It's meant to come to Hamburg and then go on to Western and Northern Europe, on a massive scale. Someone wants to build solid structures, east-west distribution channels. They're not there for this stuff yet. But they soon will be.'

He looks at me. 'You can't do anything about it, it's all wrapped up already. You and your people might bust a delivery now and then, but it won't bother anyone, the structure's too big and too well constructed.'

Pause.

Cigarette.

'But that's not why I ended up in here,' he says.

I light another cigarette for myself too – feels like the seventeenth this afternoon – and look him in the eyes.

Don't cock up now.

Don't talk out of turn.

'There are three little crooks. They're just dogsbodies in the whole thing really – meant to pin a few people down, make a connection or two, get the Hamburg street business ready. But they want to do their own thing. And believe me, what they're planning is way more fucked up than everything I already told you, and worse than anything you've seen yet. The drug these guys want to bring into Germany is sick. And just to make a fast million. They've got straw for brains.'

I smoke evenly in and out so I don't forget to breathe.

'And it was those three boys,' he says, holding up his left index finger, 'that I underestimated.'

He drags on his cigarette.

'I'll tell you their names. And then I'm saying nothing else.'

The sun is about to vanish behind the hospital. I pull my coat more tightly around my body and turn up my collar. The Austrian still has exactly three rays of sunshine on his brow.

He looks to the heavens. 'Drob, Adlo and Ronny.'

'Drob, Adlo and Ronny?' I ask. 'What kind of names are they?'

'Fighting names,' he says. 'I don't know anything else about them myself.'

'You have to give me another lead,' I say. 'What drug is it? Who's behind it? What exactly are these three – what are their names again? – planning?'

'Drob. Adlo. Ronny.'

'Yeah, them. What are they planning?'

He gives one last drag on his cigarette and throws the butt away. 'Message ends.'

'Please. Joe.'

'It's cold. Take me back in.'

'You have to keep talking to me.'

'I don't have to do anything except get out of the cold. And don't even think about blackmailing me. Or I'll never speak another word to you.'

Shame. It was a good idea.

'OK,' I say. I can see there's nothing more to come.

'Forward march!'

I push him back through the door. To the lift, up to the ward, into his room.

When he's lying in bed again, his face gradually recovering from the pain of the wheelchair-to-bed campaign, I say: 'By the way, I heard you're planning to pay for all this in cash.'

He nods.

'Where did you get that kind of money? You know how expensive this stuff is, don't you?'

He looks at me. Flickering in his eyes is a healthy dose of derision.

He grins and now gives me a look like I'm a particularly dim work-experience student.

First I feel my carotid artery throbbing, then my lid flipping.

'WHO ARE YOU, JOE?'

He looks out of the window and says: 'Not so loud, if you please, ma'am.'

I drop onto the chair beside his bed. 'Just tell me how you stumbled into this business and then we can work out how to get you out again. And then it'll be fine.'

He laughs, shakes his head and says: 'Cute.'

I stand up again, walk around his bed and stand in front of the window, blocking his view.

Drob, Adlo and Ronny are doing something involving drugs, I think. Great. Give the wheelchair back, old man.

We stare at each other. First one to blink is dead.

'Do you speak Esperanto?' he asks.

'No,' I say. 'Do you?'

'A bit,' he says, continuing to hold my gaze rock solid. He's very good at it. As if he's done a course in gaze-holding. 'There's a village in the French Pyrenees where they only speak Esperanto, and they have a word there for people who abuse the rules of the community. Who harm others through antisocial behaviour.'

'What's the word?' I ask.

'Krokodili.'

'As in crocodile?'

'As in crocodile.'

'And?' I ask.

'Don't be uptight now,' he says.

'I'm not uptight,' I say. 'I've just had enough of your puzzles. This is not a fairy tale. I'm not in the mood any more. Keep your shit to yourself.'

He tries to sit up a bit, but without much success. Then he gestures towards the bedside cabinet with his head. 'Look in the drawer there,' he says.

I open it, and there's a piece of paper. On the paper, in girlish handwriting, it says '*Wieczorkowski*'.

'What's that?'

'I got one of the nurses to write it for you,' he says. 'In case anything happens to me here.'

'In case what, exactly, happens to you?'

'Whatever,' he says. 'Ask the man about crocodiles. But don't give him my regards.'

'Where will I find this Wieczorkowski?'

'At the State Criminal Police Office in Leipzig. He's one of the best narcotics detectives in this country. If anyone can help you, it's him.'

I slip the note into my trouser pocket. 'You're an oddball,' I say.

'I'm a serious drinker,' he says.

'Meaning?'

'I don't like boxing matches that are decided on points. If you mess with me, you have to assume it'll be the last time you mess with anyone.'

I don't like jogging in the park after dark. I'm not scared by a dark park, but I need points of light around me to be able to think.

And without daylight, the park is a dark-green swamp.

So I run through the Speicherstadt, the port, the Hafencity, the city centre. There are lights everywhere. And runners. A distinct species that only uses these districts at night. To run in peace through the dead streets. In fact I'm hardly ever here by day. And I reckon the others aren't either, from what I can see in their faces. The people who come in the daytime have respect in their eyes – for the old warehouses in the old warehouse district, for the swaying ships at the jetties, for the monstrous buildings in the new part of town, for the blaring shop windows in the shopping district. The people here at night just use the whole shebang as a stage for their thing. There's something noble about that. It's one of those rare moments when humanity towers above the city, when we do what we want with it, and not the other way round.

I run for a good hour – around me the red brick, the glass façades, the concrete. Above me, the sky. And in my head just Drob, Adlo and Ronny.

I'm still going slightly nuts over all these endless fighting names.

After showering, I'm dog tired; my legs are as heavy as a crane base. I could just fall into bed. But something's pulling me outside. I feel like beer and music and Klatsche. I slip into the absolute minimum of clothes, pull on my boots, snatch up my coat and let the door fall into the lock behind me before sleep catches up with me after all.

Out on the street, I latch onto the crowd heading for the Reeperbahn. I find my place between two little groups – a couple of young men in front and three women behind; they're all in step, matching tempo, a still-things-to-do-today beat. We're on our way to the Kiez.

A pleasure-seeking pack. A human wave.

I just let myself be swept along with it, wait and see where it takes me.

We turn right and then left and then keep straight on. Past phone shops, tattooists, porn cinemas and old dives, past the Salvation

Army and a travel agent's, past people laughing and people lying in doorways. Past rich and poor people, and past plenty who'll even forget their own names tonight, leave them lying around wherever they dropped them – under a sticky table or just down the loo. On the Reeperbahn, my walking group swells rapidly; it's like cell division, suddenly there's an insane number and now you seriously have to watch out that you don't dock in the wrong place. I cross the Reeperbahn, and there's clinking and clanking and clanging and jeering; dirty little Las Vegas, I think, what are you lot really looking for? And then I see a pale-blue Pontiac in front of the Silbersack.

Well, look at that. Faller. In the Silbersack tonight. Let's go and see.

The door to what must be the cutest tacky pub in Hamburg is wide open; it always is, whether it's warm or cold outside. The real barrier to events is a heavy black curtain, split down the middle. I once hid in the curtain with Klatsche back when I didn't want to kiss him in public. Standing in the doorway, and on the bit of pavement between the curtain and the street, are a few guys in dark jackets who are mostly wearing woolly hats. Bottle of beer in one hand, cigarette in the other. Right next to the door, a couple are dancing on the street to music that presumably only they can hear.

I squeeze past the men to the curtain and push it aside a little, but stay standing in the entrance. In the Silbersack, no one pays you any attention just because you push the curtain aside. You have to go to the bar if you want something.

Faller is at the bar, talking. Hands in his trouser pockets, shoulders back, belly out. His hat sits perkily on his head; his trench coat is pushed slightly back: all in all, he has a very jaunty air. On the bar in front of him are a packet of Roth-Händle and a lighter; a cigarette glows in the ashtray; next to the ashtray is a bottle of beer.

I'd really like to hear what Faller's saying, but the music's too loud. A punk version of 'Goodbye Johnny' that's not even that bad.

I sidle a little closer to Faller and hide about two metres from him, behind a rather expansive old woman with a large white hat. She smells of cigarettes, schnapps and lily of the valley. I sit diagonally behind her on a bench; my view of Faller is blocked by a thin wooden panel, but that means he can't see me either if he turns round. I can still only hear 'Goodbye Johnny', though – the jukebox is just too loud. And sometimes one punter or other bawls something equally punk that doesn't have much to do with the lyrics.

Then I get lucky. Apparently the jukebox wasn't properly fed. Once the song's over, nothing follows it. A girl with pretty, light-blue hair is the first to notice; she throws in a handful of change, taking care of music supplies, a bottle of beer in her hand. It's not an easy task, takes a moment – she's not very steady on her feet.

And I, behind the fat, lily-of-the-valley woman, can hear Faller telling the people at the bar: '…and in the end it's fair to say that the Albanian only owns a quarter of the Hafencity because he forced so many little girls' hands onto hotplates, and bribed the right senators, city councillors and public prosecutors.'

Dude.

I think I've flipped.

When he sees me outside by his Pontiac, he stops, takes his hands out of his trouser pockets and crosses them over his by now fairly considerable paunch. We look at each other across the street, and suddenly there are only the two of us in the pale light falling onto the cobbles from the single-storey Silbersack pub. Everything else has bowed out of the situation. Just vanished from my sight. I don't take in the swaying, singing, drinking Saturday-evening crowd, or the colourful lamps flashing along with the music in the windows of the Silbersack.

Faller's muttering.

Then he says: 'And? I've got this under control.'

'Like fuck you have.'

2006, autumn.

FALLER, GEORG

He's atomised me. Ripped me to shreds, shot me to dust, made me invisible. And if anyone does see me, they keep out of my way.

That's how it goes when nobody knows exactly what's happened, but everybody knows that what did happen was hardcore.

I meet the girl in the blood-soaked underwear every night in my dreams.

RILEY, CHASTITY

We went for a drink, Faller and I. And I mean a drink.

Then I keeled over. Roofies, I think. Or something of that sort.

When I woke up the next morning, on a bench next to the bar where we'd been drinking the night before, Faller wasn't there.

I found him on the first floor over the bar – the door was open; I knew I'd have to go up there.

He was lying on a bed; next to him was a girl in blood-smeared underwear. Lying on the girl was a note:

'Keep out, old man.'

I didn't know what to do, so I phoned Klatsche. He raced over, all blue lights and sirens. He took the girl away.

I held Faller's hand and called Calabretta to take Faller away.

If we ever find out who the girl was and what happened to her, perhaps it'll thaw out the ice that Faller's wrapped himself in since that night.

KLASSMAN, HENRI

My neighbour rang me. She said it was an emergency. She didn't know who else could help.

I could never have imagined an emergency that bad. There was an old copper on a bed. A dead girl beside him. He couldn't remember a thing.

My neighbour said her colleague had been shafted and had nothing to do with the girl's death.

He looked at her, and then at me. Eyes dark.

I believed them. They're good people, my neighbour and her colleague.

I phoned my granddad. He's a gravedigger out in the sticks. He sorted it. The really sad thing about it is that there's nobody to miss the girl, at least not here in Germany.

CALABRETTA, VITO

The chief was sitting on the edge of that bed.

That hideous bed. Covered in muck and blood.

He was sitting there. Collapsed. As if he'd met the devil himself.

I helped him up, led him out through the storm raging that morning, sat him in my car and drove him home. He didn't want to get out.

Two hours we sat in that car, him staring at his front door. As if the thing that had happened would only come true if he moved. If he opened his front door and let it into his life.

I don't know exactly what happened. I don't ask either.

It's like the boss is deep-frozen.

VELOSA, CARLA

When I asked old Faller if he wanted a beer, he looked at me like I'd offered him a couple of teenage whores on toast.

I'm not drinking again, he said. Never again.

I wonder what happened.
Nobody tells me anything.

MALUTKI, ROCCO

I was home in Hamburg for a while. A difficult place right now.
There's nothing for me there but trouble.

Had a few beers with Klatsche.

He's got worries too. Didn't want to talk about it though.

I'm going on to Buenos Aires.

JOE

That was a nasty thing he did.

You don't do that stuff.

MALAJ, GJERGJ

People always find it so hard to kill women.

No women, no kids, blahblahblah.

But they're the easiest. And you can do such interesting things
with them.

Maybe the lot of them will simmer down now.

BECAUSE IT'S SUNDAY

We're sitting by the Elbe. To my left is Calabretta, to my right is Klatsche; they're both tired in their own way. We're sitting on wooden chairs, wrapped in blankets, noses in the sun, feet in the sand. The water makes little waves on the shore; now and then, a ship passes by. In front of us are three half-full bottles of beer and three empty plates, which, half an hour ago, still held three portions of soused herrings and fried potatoes.

It's Sunday.

And we're three people off on a day out.

Earlier, on the ferry, I told Calabretta about last night. About my encounter with Faller. He looked mildly impressed and nodded presidentially now and again, but that was his only reaction.

We all swig our beer; the men go: 'Aah!'

I look over at Klatsche. He's got his eyes closed, he's smiling. A gull is hopping around his feet, squawking quietly to itself.

'Do the names Drob, Adlo and Ronny mean anything to you?' I ask him.

He keeps his eyes shut. 'Ex-colleagues from the old days. Why?'

'Ex-colleagues? What does that mean?'

'We cracked a few phone shops together,' he says, eyes still shut. As if that were nothing. That time we cracked a few phone shops. 'But then, well, you know, it all went a bit wrong for me. And when I got out of jail, the boys had gone into drugs. And I didn't want to go there. And anyway…' He pauses briefly and blinks at me. His eyes glitter bright green. '…I turned respectable not long after.'

He drinks more beer. 'What do you want from them then?'

'I would very much like to know their real names,' I say. 'Because I need to ask those gentlemen a question.'

'Not a clue,' he says, raising his face to the sun again.

That's a lie. Klatsche knows everything about guys he's done jobs with.

'Come on,' I say. 'It's about the man in the hospital. I'm not getting anywhere. Those three are all I've got.'

'What have those boys got to do with it?' he asks, and I think I can hear a hint of something lurking in his voice.

'That's what I'd like to know.'

That's all I say. Anything he can do, I could do years ago.

'I'll listen out,' he says.

Like hell he will. I'll have to chew on granite a bit longer. But I'm good at chewing on granite. Klatsche knows that, which is why he turns up the collar of his leather jacket. To protect himself from my chewing apparatus.

I glance left at Calabretta because I'm starting to wonder why he's not contributing anything.

Ah. He's fallen asleep.

And the gull that was busy around Klatsche just now has settled on his shoulder.

I drink up my beer, lay my hand on Klatsche's forearm and say: 'Well, see you three later.'

'Where're you going?'

'To see the next man who won't talk to me,' I say, and I don't mean the Austrian, but Faller.

But this time, I call first.

Faller leaves the Pontiac in a side street.

'I don't like hospital car parks,' he says. 'If you're so weak you have to park directly outside the hospital, you might as well check into the place right away.'

There it is again – Faller's midlife crisis. He must be properly scared of getting old. Watching the spring in his step as he crosses the road, there's really no need for it.

He's still a man who leads the way.

And he seems to be interested in my Austrian, Joe. While we were still in the car he asked exactly which room he was in, and now, as the hospital entrance comes into view, he almost breaks into a run. He is, and always will be, a cop, and he doesn't stop till he gets to the door of Joe's room, where the policeman is sitting on his chair, reading the Sunday paper.

'Mornin'' says Faller, rocking from his heels to his tiptoes and back again.

'Mornin'' says the policeman, smiling and looking at me.

'It's all right,' I say. 'I thought I'd bring a gentleman visitor this time.'

'All right then,' says the policeman, burying his head in the paper again.

The front-page news is that one of the old Kiez bosses has had a heart attack. One of the biggest. I hope Faller doesn't see it – that would only stoke his current condition.

But he went into the room ages ago, without knocking or messing about.

'Hello,' he says, taking a chair and sitting down by Joe's bed.

I stay standing behind the chair and say: 'A friend of mine. A little male company for a change. And because it's Sunday.'

'Oh, it's Sunday, is it?' says Joe, nodding thoughtfully and looking over my old friend as if he has X-ray eyes.

Then he says: 'Mr Faller. There's a thing.'

Do you two know each other? I'd like to ask.

Or: What's up?

Or: I beg your pardon?

But I'm utterly speechless.

Faller isn't.

'Have we met?' he asks, pulling his I'll-whip-out-my-notepad-in-a-minute face.

Joe shakes his head. 'No,' he says, 'we've never met. But I know you.'

Recently, when it was still winter.

FALLER, GEORG

He wanted me to die of my grief, my questions, my doubts. But I didn't die. I cheated. I went numb. I put myself on ice.

There are stories of injured men in glacier crevasses. What the body does is, it drives down your temperature, your metabolism and everything, and waits.

Some even hang on till they're rescued.

My rescue was that one of his little runners squealed – admitted that he'd put the dead girl in my bed and that I hadn't touched her. Since then, I've been able to look at my daughter without thinking about that girl every damn time.

The girl isn't on my conscience. I couldn't have saved her; I couldn't have prevented anything – it happened to me.

There's enough on my conscience anyway – Minou's been lying there for almost thirty years.

All the same, I'd made peace with that in recent years. With everything.

It won't do any good, I thought.

Now I know that was cowardly. That it means I'd made peace with the Albanian, and making peace with him is not an option. You have to fight people like that, all your life.

I'd just forgotten. I was sleeping like an old man. A dull old goat.

But then there was that New Year reception at the Town Hall. I remember not wanting to go, but my wife persuaded me. Something about new experiences. And then that.

Suddenly that bastard appears next to me.

He sees me, recognises me. He's standing with a few guys who think they're fine gentlemen. Some of them are, officially at least.

What does that arsehole do? Orders a whole round of drinks from me.

They all know I'm not a waiter. They all laugh. What's the joke, exactly?

And suddenly I heard the shot again.

Suddenly I realised: you can't let those guys sit on you, Faller. If he thought I wasn't an enemy any more, he was mistaken.

MALAJ, GJERGJ

This city has done its duty. Hafencity's up and running, and it pays. We're moving soon. To Eastern Europe.

Then Hamburg's only job will be to help milk the west for a bit more.

Ways and means are the name of the game in good business.

An organism is only healthy when the blood vessels are working properly.

And the blood vessels are working properly when the money gets to me in the end.

DROST, PAUL

This evening.

ADELMANN, NICO

First delivery.

NIEHUS, ROBERT

We're big.
Really big.

JOE

I was almost sure that the old cop had hanged himself. Or gone into a loony bin, at least.

But suddenly there he was, at my bedside.

ZIMMERMANN, SUNNY

C'mon, give me the gear.

Hurry up.

I want to forget about yesterday.

And the day before.

Most of all, I'd like to forget my whole life.

STENGER, JAKOB

Of course.

And if you do forget everything: I'm in.

NOW IT'S BROKEN

'Hello, West Saxony Narcotics Investigation Team.'

A friendly but tired female voice.

'Riley, Hamburg State Prosecution Department, hello. Could I speak to Mr Wieczorkowski, please?'

'What's it regarding?'

'I'm afraid I don't really know that myself,' I say.

I walk over to the open window, that narrow thing, and light a cigarette. 'An informant advised me to talk to Mr Wieczorkowski.'

'OK, one moment please.'

Click.

Ring.

'Wieczorkowski.'

'Riley, Hamburg State Prosecution Department. Hello, Mr Wieczorkowski. I'm glad you really exist.'

'Why shouldn't I exist?'

His voice is deep and it sounds like he's laughing as he speaks.

'There's someone on my hands,' I say, 'who talks in riddles. And your name came up in one of them. I wasn't quite sure what to make of it.'

'And what's this somebody's name?'

'No idea. He calls himself Joe. He's Austrian, and I was specifically not to give you his regards.'

There's a pause for thought at the other end of the line.

Then: 'What did he say about why you should call me?'

'I should ask you about crocodiles,' I say, hoping he doesn't laugh, or just put the phone down on me.

'He mentioned crocodiles?' asks Wieczorkowski.

'He did.'

'In what context?'

'I'm not quite sure of that myself. He talked about Esperanto. But I think it's really about drugs, if I've understood correctly.'

'Did he talk about crocodiles in Hamburg?'

'I couldn't say – I only followed about half of it. What is all this about crocodiles?'

Wieczorkowski doesn't answer. But I can hear him thinking again.

'Do you have time to come and see me in Leipzig?'

'When?' I ask.

'Pack your bag, get on the next train. I'll meet you at the station. Wait … The next train from Hamburg to Leipzig goes in just under an hour. Can you make that?'

'Now you wait,' I say.

'I'm waiting.'

'Can't we discuss this on the phone?'

'I don't like discussing things by phone,' he says. 'I grew up in the GDR.'

'The GDR no longer exists,' I say.

'The technology does though.'

'I'm small fry,' I say. 'It's not worth tapping me.'

'I'd be worth it, though,' he says. 'How about it? Do you want to talk to me?'

'Yes,' I say. 'I do.'

'Then get on the train.'

'OK,' I say. 'Er, well then, we'll do that. Thank you for the time-table information.'

'*Da nich für,*' he says. 'Don't mention it.'

'That's what they say in Hamburg…' I say.

'I spent a while in your city as a young man. That was a long time ago now. See you later then, Ms … What was your name?'

'Riley,' I say.

'OK, Ms Riley.'

'OK, Mr Wieczorkowski.'

I hang up and call Faller. I ask him to keep an eye on the Austrian for a day or two because I've got to go away. I tell him that I wouldn't mind if he got anything out of him, as they clearly have some kind of connection.

I leave my sickly office, take a taxi home, pack a bag, head for the station and wonder if this is really so wise, but what can you do?

The fog is travelling into East Germany with us. Under the fog, and in its holes, are fields and meadows. In them are old, isolated trees bearing mistletoe. Now and again there's a scrap of woodland.

It's a bit like travelling through another time, a time about 150 years ago maybe, before the twentieth century came, bringing its wars and all that madness, at the end of which was the barking-mad twenty-first century. The landscape outside the window is peaceful, self-contained. A couple of deer here, a stream there; in the centre of the image is an old farmhouse.

Every time one of those mail-order housing estates pops up, or an industrial park, or an enormous supermarket, or a solar farm, my eyes get a shock. As if a bomb has gone off in the middle of the picture. And every time my eyes get a shock, it reminds me of my failed country break. I still don't know what I was doing there, but it gave me a similar feeling. Except that it was me who had blown up the picture. I was the eyesore.

Perhaps it's always like that. Whenever I wish for something, whenever I imagine how something could be, that's bound to be the moment it falls to bits.

In Berlin, a dozen loud teenage girls from Munich get in. Every one of them has long, blonde plaits, tiny, expensive jackets, checked scarves and gold earrings. Their voices are as shrill as if they've been eating neon chalk. A horde of screeching Barbies. And they sit right behind me all the way to Leipzig.

Crocodiles, I think, and have no idea where to go with that.

*

He's standing at the end of platform 13, holding a scrap of card; on the card it says: '*Riley Hamburg*'.

'That must be me,' I say, holding my right hand out to him.

First he takes my hand, then he takes my bag, saying: 'Welcome to the wild east. I'm Hannes.'

'I'm Chastity.'

'What? Cassidy?'

'You can call me Riley.'

'OK,' he says. 'Riley – maybe that's easier.'

He looks at me like people always do when my first name is under discussion – somewhere between bewildered and amused.

He's a hell of a guy. Must be about six foot two, aged around fifty. He looks good. OK, so his hairline's retreated quite a way and his skin looks like it's got far too much sun over the years, but he must have been a very handsome man once. He has one of those chiselled faces, his eyes glint a dark blue, he has enormously broad shoulders and under his hiking jacket I can't see even a hint of a belly. His long brown hair is tied in a little bun on the back of his head. Nobody ought to be able to get away with that, but on him it works. Put it this way: a few feathers on his head and he'd be a Sioux chieftain.

Outside the station he offers me a cigarette. 'Start with a smoke?'

'Please,' I say taking one of his organic fags. Sky-blue box with a smoking Indian on it. Sioux. I knew it.

Ah. Smoke.

'What's that sad old bunker?' I ask.

Right opposite the station is a dark-grey, stucco-decorated building. The windows are boarded up; the façade up to first-floor level has been taken over by rather unimaginative graffiti.

'Used to be Walter Ulbricht's favourite hotel,' says Wieczorkowski. 'The cellar's been flooded since the water table rose. They pump it out round the clock. Belated after-effect of lignite mining.'

He does up his jacket, ciggie in the corner of his mouth, eyes front. 'Now, why don't you tell me what's going on over there in Hamburg?'

'I hope you can tell me that. I'm up to my knees in mysteries.'

'What about the Austrian informant you've reeled in?'

'He's been in hospital a week because three guys broke all his bones and cut off his right index finger,' I say. 'Since then, I've been trying to find out who he is and what exactly happened. On Saturday, out of the blue, he came up with your name.'

'What does this man look like, then?' he asks.

'He's tall,' I say, 'mid to late forties, maybe. Angular face, silver-grey hair.'

Wieczorkowski nods, but more to himself, then he says: 'Why do you know it's about drugs?'

'He told me that was why he was beaten up.'

'And that's all you know?'

'That's all I know.'

I've forgotten the names Drob, Adlo and Ronny, just to be on the safe side. I have a rule: don't trust anyone I've only known for ten minutes.

'OK,' he says. 'Well, let's go for a walk. I'll show you something.'

We set off, still smoking. We walk past the broken hotel and turn down a quiet side street, and I find myself thinking that Leipzig looks like any other medium-sized German city, only a bit better. Tidy in a Bavarian kind of way. Pretty. Old. Picture-book. Listed buildings everywhere.

We come to a tree-lined square that looks like it was smartened up with nail scissors. A church. Houses with bay windows and mini onion domes. Lattice windows as far as the eye can see. To our right is a large sandstone building, maybe from the turn of the last century, or perhaps a bit later – what do I know? Wieczorkowski heads for a wooden bench under a tree.

'Have a seat,' he says, looking at the church clock. It's almost half past two. 'It's nearly time.'

We sit down. We've got a perfect view of the big building.

'Is that a school?' I ask.

He nods. 'A grammar school,' he says. 'Gets some of the best results in the city. You see the long fence to the right of the school?'

Behind the fence is a cluster of small trees and tall bushes, ever-green stuff.

'What about it?' I ask.

'Keep your eye on it,' he says. 'It won't be long now.'

We light cigarettes and smoke.

'Now,' he says.

Three young men have suddenly appeared by the fence. They look like students – wearing thick hoodies and crumpled shoulder bags, which don't seem to have much in them. They could also be youth workers or young teachers. The next moment, the school's large double doors fly open and the teenagers plunge out into the abyss: they ought to spread like wildfire across the square and dis-perse into their free time, like you do when school's over, but they don't.

Following some internal system, they form into little groups and walk past the fence. They each stop by one of the men in hoodies. Swap something. One for you, one for me. Then they turn the corner. And they're gone.

After barely two minutes, it's all over. Nobody there, not even the guys with the bags.

Wieczorkowski looks at me.

'What was that?' I ask.

'Meth,' he says.

'Crystal meth?'

He nods and says: 'The usual.'

'Why don't you do something about it?'

'My colleagues can be at ten schools at a time, max,' he says. 'We don't have any more people. But every school in this town has a fence like that. With at least forty secondary schools, you can imagine the job we have.'

'I see,' I say.

What I find so hard to imagine is how ordinary the meth thing clearly is here. Neither Wieczorkowski nor the students nor the dealers by the fence seem all that concerned. Just ordinary.

'They didn't look like freaks,' I say. 'They looked like fresh-faced, healthy teenagers.'

'The freaks live on the edge of society,' he says. 'In the holes and sometimes at the station. The freaks are the rats that eat the drug rubbish. If you're middle class and can afford the good stuff, you can keep it together for quite a while before it breaks you.' He drags on his cigarette and looks up to the sky. 'And until then, you're the king of your little world. Don't need to sleep or eat, you're always at the top of your game, you can party all weekend and look amazing while you're at it.'

He looks at me. 'Basically, with meth in your blood, you're this world's exact ideal: slim and quick and always wide awake.'

'No,' I say.

'Yes,' he says. 'Think about it, Riley.'

If that's the case, slim is about all I've got to offer.

'Where does all the stuff sold here come from?'

'The Czech Republic,' he says. 'A good hour's drive. You can buy as much as you like there.'

The Czech Republic.

From Hamburg that seems hideously far away. A couple of hours by train to Leipzig and suddenly you're very close by.

'Shall we drive over there?'

'Sure,' he says. 'But first I want to show you something else.'

We go back towards the station. In a side street, we get into a white Ford Transit with tinted windows. A monster.

'What is this?' I ask. 'A mobile TV studio?'

'Bit eye-catching, I know,' he says, shrugging. 'But every dealer within a two-hundred-K radius knows me anyway, and the junkies know who I am too. Which is bad for stake-outs, but the advantage is I can drive whatever car I like. And I like this old, white juggernaut.'

'How long have you been doing this job?'

'Almost fifteen years.' He straps himself in and turns the ignition key. 'Before that, I was on the drugs squad in Hamburg.'

'No way,' I say.

'Yes way,' he says, accelerating.

*

On the edge of town, a dozen gloomy people are cowering by the wall of a building that looks like an abandoned railway waiting room with broken windows. Their faces are white and shiny, their eyes are dark and guttering, they're all scarily thin. Now and again one stands up and power walks up and down. Then cowers against the wall again.

The wall is about to shatter under the weight of so much misery.

'Here you go,' says Wieczorkowski. 'Here are your freaks.'

'Thank you very much,' I say.

I can hardly look.

He stops the engine and undoes his seat belt. 'Come with me for a moment.'

We get out and walk past the living corpses; we might as well step over them. It feels so awful to just abandon people like that.

We enter a small tunnel next to the tumbledown building. It's dark and damp inside; I can hear rustling and scurrying, and I see long, thin tails.

Animals. Lots of animals.

On the far side of the tunnel we turn left and stop outside what used to be toilets, and inside, in a corridor, a couple are lying. They look terrible; they really are living corpses – the meth victims back there had lovely complexions in comparison. The pallor of these two is verging on greenish; they look like how kids draw zombies: not meant to be all that hideous but they still turned out that way.

The zombies are just lying there. No idea how old they are. Their faces are sunken. There are green ulcers on their hands, on their arms and on their necks.

'That's krok,' says Wieczorkowski. 'Also known as krokodil.'

I can't move and I can't speak. I want: to scream. To cry.

This is just wrong.

'It's one of the worst things on the market. Codeine tablets cooked up with formic acid and match heads. At first it's like heroin – gives you an incredible high – but it's much, much cheaper than heroin, and much more brutal. One shot costs two euros fifty.'

I'd like to say something now; I ought to say something, but my throat is squeezed shut.

'Most of them are dead in six months,' says Wieczorkowski. 'And withdrawal takes a whole month and hurts so much that they need tranquilisers or they keep passing out from the pain. So hardly anyone ever gets off it. An American newspaper once wrote that krok was the most horrific drug in the world. I'm telling you – this is meth's cousin from hell.'

'We have to call an ambulance,' I whisper. 'An ambulance, please.'

'We will,' he says. 'But in a week or two they'll be back here, believe me.'

I take a deep breath.

For a moment, I'd forgotten to breathe.

Wieczorkowski takes me by the arm and shepherds me back to the Transit. I can hardly put one leg in front of the other.

He puts me in the van and calls the paramedics.

I pay no attention to where we're driving. I have no idea where I am or what the time is.

In my head are mini forklifts, busy sorting the images onto secret shelves that I won't be able to get to quickly. In a day or two, we'll see if it's worked.

After a while, I find my voice again.

'And you think that's what my informant meant by crocodiles?'

'Yes, I think so,' he says. 'In fact, I'm sure of it. I know your informant.'

I look at him sideways; he's watching the road, notices that I'm looking at him but doesn't react.

Eventually he says: 'I'll explain, I promise, but later; I need two or three beers for that. Or five.'

'I'd be happy to go for a beer right now,' I say.

'So would I,' he says, 'but you wanted to go to the Czech side, didn't you?'

Wanted isn't the word for it.

But work is work and schnapps is schnapps.

We drive through an idyllic slice of eastern Germany. Small, colourful houses, slender trees, languid fields. White wooden benches under lanky birches or old weeping willows. And every now and then, some more abandoned industry. An old foundry or a brickworks or a hangar or a whatever-factory in crumbling brick. Windows with trees where the glass should be, which always looks a bit like there's a fairy-tale castle in the pipeline.

I try to fill my mind with it, to pour in something white and soapy, but unfortunately it's already full. The crocodile couple are filling it to the brim. I don't think tidying them onto the secret shelves is going to work.

Wieczorkowski stares at the road. He said we'd talk later over beer. If that's how it is, that's how it is, and that's fine by me.

After Dresden the idyll's over. It's almost a relief. Idyll on top of horror just intensifies the horror.

We drive through long, dark valleys.

'Arthritis valleys,' says Wieczorkowski, and looking at the faces of the few people out and about here, I immediately know what he means. Life here hurts, and not just in the joints. We drive through villages called Elend and Oberpöbel: 'Misery' and 'Upper Rabble'. We drive through a larch wood; at first the trees get greyer and greyer with every metre, then suddenly they're dead. Buckle over the ground, grow down instead of up; and if they're not dead yet, they're hideously maimed.

'For God's sake,' I say.

'Nitrate salts,' says Wieczorkowski, 'blowing over the border, over the hill, for decades.'

There's snow on the hilltop. Grey, naturally.

Beyond the hilltop, the view opens out; I can see as far as the next grey hilltop, the next valley, but there's nothing anywhere here either. Borderland; impenetrable for so long, and now forgotten. As if it weren't even there.

The road leads steeply down from the hilltop. The first thing I see is an unwelcoming sign standing idly, a blot on the landscape: Konzum. Behind it is a string of barns – white-grey, single-storey narrow sheds with tiny windows. Standing outside are solitary men in dark clothes, Asians with sullen faces. Arrayed in rows outside the doors are products that can be bought in the barn behind. Outsized garden gnomes. Hanging baskets. Jogging suits.

'Who buys this stuff?' I ask, and Wieczorkowski says: 'Nobody comes here to buy garden gnomes. The meth kitchens are maybe ten minutes' drive away. If you want to buy something, you tell these gentlemen and one of them drives off, and half an hour later, the stuff changes hands.'

'And krok?' I ask. 'Can you get that here too?'

'If it'll kill you, you can get it here,' he says. 'But we don't know much about krok. It's still very rare at home. We just know it's there. It comes from Russia and it's slowly eating its way westwards.'

'Like a crocodile?'

'Like a crocodile.'

He's slowed down – we're more or less creeping from barn to barn. Before very long, three to five men are standing outside every door, watching our van.

'You see,' he says. 'They know me.'

He pulls two cigarettes from the glove compartment, gives me one and lights the other for himself. He opens the window a crack.

'Of course they also know that I can't do a thing,' he says, dragging on his cigarette. 'I'm completely reliant on my colleagues on this side of the border.'

He passes me his lighter.

'And?' I ask.

'We work closely together,' he says; 'and we're getting better.'

'Why are there these markets? Can't anyone just shut them down?'

'You tell that to the mayors of these godforsaken villages here.

The Vietnamese markets are basically their only functional economic structure. And everyone makes a little something from it.'

'Corruption,' I say.

'I don't want to piss off my Czech colleagues,' he says. 'They're doing their best. And like this, at least we can keep an eye on it. Can watch it. Battery farming, you know?'

He glances outside. Meets the eyes of all the men outside the barns. They're on the verge of nodding to each other. There've been years where they've been unpleasantly chained together. A sticky relationship.

The internal coldness of this relationship is one of the frostiest things I've ever felt.

Wieczorkowski puts the heating on.

'Cold here,' he says.

And I think: battery farming.

Dresden Neustadt. A bit like a miniature version of Berlin twenty years ago. We stand at a heavy bar, waiting for our first beer. To shorten the ten-to-twenty-second wait, the barman has already given us two vodkas.

'At the Ost-Pol,' Wieczorkowski said earlier, when I asked him the best place to get a few beers. 'Like the North or South Poles, but in the east.'

I can't think of a name that would suit this place better. Clear and uncompromising and dark and glorious and perfectly off-beat. The predominant colours are light brown, dark brown, and orange, or all at once, preferably in decades-old wavy or checked patterns. All the men have untrimmed beards; lots of them are wearing peculiar caps. A punk band is playing in the room next door. They're torturing their guitars; a woman with a very loud and very sad voice sings: 'Now it's broken'.

Everyone's smoking. We down the vodka. Then come two bottles of beer.

'Your health, Chastity,' says Wieczorkowski.

'Cheers, Hannes.'

We toast each other and drink.

The cigarette smoke wreathes around our heads, enveloping us and comforting me. The vodka warms me from inside out.

Wieczorkowski stares at the wall behind the bar. 'Do you have kids?'

I shake my head.

'I've got two sons,' he says. 'They're eleven and thirteen. And whenever I stand outside a school like we did this afternoon, watching that parade, I can't sleep for a couple of nights.'

'Shall we sit here all night then?'

'If you like,' he says. 'But I booked a hotel room for you, just round the corner.'

'Thanks,' I say.

'No problem,' he says, gulping his beer.

'How often do you watch the parade?'

'Too often.'

He devotes his attention to his jacket sleeve, flips it over and back again.

'Have you been outside your boys' school?'

He nods. 'But they go to school here, because they live with their mother,' he says. 'It's not quite as bad in Dresden. Leipzig's definitely got it worse.'

'Why?'

He shrugs. 'Dresden's stuffy. Not much happens apart from in this little area. Leipzig's full of parties and clubs. Stuff like that spreads faster there.'

He finishes his beer and orders two more. I hurry to catch up. And another two vodkas.

'Cheers.'

'Cheers.'

The woman next door sings that it's broken now for one last time, then the concert's over.

'Don't you live with your family?' I ask.

'Sometimes yes, sometimes no,' he says. 'I've got a room in Leipzig and a small flat in Dresden. And sometimes I'm together with them all in the big flat. My wife and I have seen better days.'

He flags down another vodka and clings onto his empty beer bottle until the shot glass comes.

'The gloss comes off even true love eventually.'

I drain my bottle. Perhaps that's why I've never had a true love. So there's no gloss to come off. Everything's rusty from the start with me.

'Everything's rusty from the start with me,' I say and then the new beers come and Wieczorkowski downs his vodka and starts laughing, and the barman takes our empty bottles from the bar and says: 'That would make a great song for our house band.'

We clink bottles and drink, and once the barman's stopped paying us any attention, Wieczorkowski slips a little closer to me and says: 'This Austrian in your hospital in Hamburg…'

'Yes?'

'There's something I need to explain.'

I look at him. His profile hardens.

'He's my confidential source.'

I choke on my beer.

Cough.

'Sorry?'

'We've known each other since my time in Hamburg,' he says, staring at his hands.

I stare at my hands too and carry on coughing because I don't know what else to do. Or what to say. I decide on: 'Oh.'

A thin strand has worked loose from his knot of hair. He strokes it slowly out of his face, as if he's playing for time.

'Who is the man?' I ask.

'A ghost,' says Wieczorkowski. 'There are very few people who even know he exists. And probably nobody who knows his real name.'

'Do you know it?'

He shakes his head; the hair falls down again. 'He's a hitman.'

A hitman.

In my head, a few jigsaw pieces shift position, and I quickly try to make a picture out of them, but I can't do it.

'You hired a hitman as a grass?'

He takes a huge swig of beer. 'Not officially. It just happened.'

It just happened. Right. And it just happened that the man I've spent a week feeling responsible for isn't a victim but a perpetrator, and a high-calibre one at that – probably in both senses of the expression. The jigsaw pieces start whirling, a carousel ride through the last few days starts up, and during the ride, piece after piece drops into place. The black suit. The workmanlike, cynical, sordid view of the world. The stupid mysteries and silence. Everything about that tough old bloke. The chopped-off index finger: the three guys wanted to really screw him over, to fuck with the trigger for ever; but they were sadly misinformed.

And then all that stuff about paying the hospital bill in cash.

My jaw drops. You could probably hear it.

Wieczorkowski looks at me with a gaze that speaks of sympathy – for me, for him, for us both and for this whole weird situation we've found ourselves in. But maybe it's only badly packaged amusement. Right at this moment, I'm not in a fit state to assess anything; it's as if I'm up a mast in a basket and looking down, and I'm about to fall, and there's absolutely nothing down there.

'Obviously, I'm perfectly well aware that it's anything but legit,' he says. 'But he's not working as a hitman any more. He's retired, however stupid that sounds. And he was the best line I could get. The man had premium information, and he shared it with me.'

'What kind of information?'

'All kinds,' he says. 'Drug stuff going down in the Hamburg underworld. Structures, distribution channels, involvements. Your colleagues on the narcotics squad did very well out of it – I often had a good tip-off for them.'

Beside me, a woman squirms her way to the bar and orders four Polish rockets, whatever they are.

'Why did Joe do that for you?' I ask, once the woman's withdrawn with four little red shots on a tray. 'He must have had a bloody good reason, mustn't he?'

'Oh, he did, believe me,' he says, turning the melody in his voice down to zero and waving to the barman. For vodka. Or maybe to say: stop asking questions, woman.

'OK,' I say.

'OK,' he says.

We drink our vodka and wait for everything to settle a bit. Which is good for the jigsaw carousel in my head.

After a while, Wieczorkowski starts again.

'I last heard from Joe ten days ago. He said something about a big crystal deal between the Czech Republic and Hamburg. He was sure that something was about to happen. But he kept it very vague – it was all hints; he wouldn't or couldn't say anything else. A couple of days ago, I tried to get hold of him again. I didn't know until this morning that anything had happened to him.'

'Now you do,' I say, lighting a cigarette. 'Do you happen to know anything about his life insurance in Switzerland?'

Wieczorkowski looks at me. 'Did he tell you about that?'

'He mentioned something along those lines,' I say, 'while explaining why he didn't need a guard on his door.'

'Hmm.'

Wieczorkowski swigs his beer.

Thinks.

'So,' he says. 'There's a bank box in Switzerland that presumably has some rather unsavoury things in it. I know that, and so do the few people who could be a danger to him. If Joe doesn't contact me for longer than four weeks, I can have the box opened.'

'Which bank?' I ask.

'I'd find out at the time,' he says, putting down his beer bottle and heading for the loo.

He can't really believe that I believe that he doesn't know which bank Joe's life insurance is in. He can't really believe that.

I try to keep him in sight but all I see is the toilet door clicking shut behind him.

He's already out of beer again.

I drink mine up too and order two more.

They land on the bar at precisely the moment that Wieczorkowski gets back.

'Very thoughtful,' he says, clattering his bottle against mine.

He notices that I'm miffed.

'What would you actually do if you knew which bank is looking after Joe's bits of paper?' he asks. 'March in with a search warrant and play Rambo?'

I shrug.

'There's no need to know everything, Riley,' he says, taking another swig from his bottle of beer. 'You only need to know the things that make a difference.'

'Such as?'

'Your people on the Hamburg drug squad have been aware of the potential meth deal for a while, and so have our colleagues in Prague. We're waiting, and we've got all our feelers out.'

He twists the beer bottle in his hand, puckers his lips a bit, his jaw bones move. He looks more wiry and angular than before; he looks like he's in battle mode – there's a little light and a little shadow falling on his face. It looks as though the Sioux chief has put his war paint on.

'OK, so tell me what I need to know about the Czech Republic and crystal.'

'The more people lose their inner self,' he says, 'the more vulnerable they are to drugs. At the moment, it seems to me that our society is pretty fragile. Believe me, if we don't watch out, we'll be overrun by it.'

'More than all the other shit?' I ask.

'You can earn so much more money with synthetic drugs than

with all the other shit,' he says. 'The Vietnamese clans now have semi-industrial kitchens ready to go; just one kitchen can produce twenty kilos of meth a day. The base material is ephedrine, which they get for free from chemists because it's available cheaply without a prescription in the Czech Republic, and because the people in the chemist's get a cut. The Vietnamese then sell a gram of meth for twenty euros. In Dresden it costs fifty; in Leipzig it's sixty; it's eighty in Berlin; and by the time you get to Hamburg, it's a hundred. Now you do the maths.'

'Can't. Too much beer.'

'If you sell the produce of a single kitchen in the Czech Republic, you'll make four hundred thousand euros a day. If you sell it in Hamburg, you make two million. A day.'

'It makes sense to get the stuff to Hamburg.'

'Put it this way: five hours clenching your arse equals five hundred per cent profit.'

He looks at me. The light flickers on his face.

War paint.

'How many of these kitchens are over there?' I ask.

'We don't know exactly,' he says. 'Doesn't matter. Dig one out and three new ones grow. It's a Hydra. There are eighteen Vietnamese markets and each market probably has two or three kitchens. Shall we do more sums?'

I shake my head; I just don't want to know, but Wieczorkowski blasts my ears with it.

'That makes, at a rough estimate, seventy-two million euros a day. So now you know why the Czech mayors in the godforsaken border areas don't shut the markets down, and why everyone else closes both their eyes to it.'

I keep shaking my head and drink more beer.

What else can I do?

'And because you've got to sell all that stuff somewhere, and Germany's too small, you need to open up a bigger market. Western Europe, for example.'

'No,' I say, maybe thinking that might stop what's coming next.

'Yes,' he says. 'And with the Port of Hamburg as the trading centre.'

'Joe hinted at something like that, but I didn't take it seriously. I didn't know who he was, after all…' I say, noticing that my voice is tailing off. 'Where would a crystal-meth business like that be managed from? From the Czech side? By the Vietnamese?'

Wieczorkowski shakes his head. 'The Vietnamese mafia doesn't generally operate across national borders. It'll probably be built up from Hamburg.'

'Who could do a job like that?' I ask, and I'm really thinking aloud, because I know the answer a second before Wieczorkowski gives it.

'Does the name Gjergj Malaj mean anything to you?'

He orders two vodkas. Just beating me to it.

'One of Malaj's nephews runs several hotels and a large casino in Prague,' he says. 'So there are plenty of contacts, infrastructure and money-laundering facilities already available.'

The vodka comes; we knock it back.

'Of course it could all be coincidence,' says Wieczorkowski. 'Or I could be going mad. But do you know what, Riley?'

'What?'

'It's just the perfect dose of fuck-up for this world.'

I look at him; his face and the scenery blur before my eyes, and I'm not sure if that's just the vodka.

'And krok?' I ask.

'Krok kills quickly,' he says. 'It doesn't quite fit the business model.'

Lovely little hotel. My room is in a kind of summerhouse in the rear courtyard. The cobblestones mingle with the ivy, and the ivy with the cobblestones.

I lie on the bed; I stare at the ceiling; God knows how long that lasts, but at some point it gets light.

The next morning.

ZIMMERMANN, SUNNY

I was behind the old station a moment ago. Now I'm here where everything looks so white.

They picked us up.

I didn't hear a blue light. Not worth it for us. But they still pick us up now and then. I guess someone keeps calling them.

There's a tube in me. Wonder where they got it in. It's really hard for me to get anything in these days.

Really hard.

Ah. Here. On the neck. There's the tube.

Don't pull, says someone, taking my hand away.

A guy, I think. Can't see him. Only the voice. Only the white light everywhere.

I'll close the curtains for you, says the guy.

And if it hurts too bad, tell me and you can have some more, OK?

OK, I think.

Jakob, I say.

Your friend's in the ICU, he says, but it'll be all right.

It'll be all right. Sure. Yeah. Right back at you.

First it's the worst fucking shit you can imagine. Then it's only half as shit. Then it's a grotesque. A monster.

It hurts like hell.

And you end up just rotting away.

I want to die, I say.

You want morphine, says the guy.

DROSTE, PAUL

All right. We're not getting our own hands dirty, are we?
    Ronny picks it up.

ADELMANN, NICO

Drob repackages it.

NIEHUS, ROBERT

Adlo passes it to his colleagues.
    The first payday should be the end of next week.

MALAJ, GJERGJ

Rang them in Italy last night. Nice weather they're having.

JOE

When you're tempted to despair…

FALLER, GEORG

…A little light comes on somewhere.

BOLTS OF RED LIGHTNING AT MY BACK

The Eurocity from Prague takes me back to Hamburg

I feel like the train is mocking me. Because I'm sure the drugs are on board too – the drugs that took me to Leipzig yesterday when I didn't have a clue what our colleagues there are up against. There might not be huge stashes of the stuff hidden between the seats, but I bet the carriages aren't clean either. After everything Wieczorkowski told me yesterday, I feel like a silly little country mouse who's been shown where things are heading.

I slump deep into the blue velvet and decide not to leave my compartment during the journey.

As we pass Leipzig, I call Faller.

He's on the move.

'Where are you, Faller?'

'Almost at the hospital,' he says. 'You asked me to keep an eye on Joe. So that's what I'm doing.'

'You can go home again,' I say. 'The guy's a hitman.'

'I know.'

'You know? How?'

'He told me.'

'Uh-huh. I see.'

'Now don't be offended, Chas.'

'What else has he told you?'

'A few anecdotes from his colourful life.'

'And did you tell him about your life too?'

'Oh. There's not much to tell there…'

'Faller?'

'Yes?'

'Kindly sod off.'

Outside the window, fields, trees and meadows flash past, and I can't handle it any more. Something's just gone spectacularly wrong.

The head of our drugs team is called Brux. He's the kind of ageing hooligan who has a bald head, five o'clock shadow and a black hoodie. His eyes glint with anger, detachment, decisiveness and something dark that always puts me in mind of Batman.

Sitting next to Brux is Tschauner; I worked with him once a few years ago. I remember that there was something puppyish about him then, and that I felt the need to protect him. And now he's sitting here amid all the real tough guys – because the drugs guys simply are the real tough ones – and the puppy's gone from his face. I wonder what happened to chase it away.

His hair is no longer so curly and freshly washed, his nose is more prominent, his eyes are deeper set.

Next to Tschauner are Messrs Kringe and Bartels. Two more old acquaintances, and better still, they're in the same boat as me – the one I'm in because of the man who lost his balls. And because it's a boat where it's good to huddle together, we're practically best friends.

I feel happier now that my first chat about this business is with people I've worked with before.

Calabretta plays football with Brux so he fits in well with the four of them.

'OK. Drob, Adlo and Ronny,' says Brux with a nod that's somewhere between meaningful and resigned. 'Paul Droste, Nico Adelmann and Robert Niehus. We certainly know them.'

'Total arses,' says Kringe, and Bartels says: 'Absolute total arses.'

Brux looks at them one at a time, and then at Tschauner, who hasn't said a thing yet.

'I'd describe them more as little arses who've been trying to make it as massive arses for years, but keep falling over their own feet. To be honest, I think they're mostly talk. Anything they touch goes to shit.'

'I can't imagine them having their fingers in a huge meth deal either,' says Tschauner.

'Even if they've only got their fingertips in it,' says Brux inspecting his nails, 'it tells us nothing more than that there *is* a deal.'

The other three rumble.

'This informant of yours and Wieczorkowski's,' says Tschauner; 'can we talk to him?'

'Tricky,' I say, thinking: I need to speak to him myself first. And to Faller. And then we'll see. The good thing about the drugs boys is that they don't kick up a fuss if you have shady, murky informers that you'd prefer not to bring too far into the light. 'Cos they all have them. Their squad probably wouldn't even exist without shadowy figures like that.

'OK,' says Brux. 'Then we'll stick closer to Drob, Adlo and Ronny.'

Of course we could always send a rapid-reaction force round to see the three gentlemen and do a DNA match on Joe's clothes and send the little arses, or big arses or whatever you want to call them, down for GBH or even attempted murder. Or we could wait and hope that Drob, Adlo and Ronny will lead us to something much bigger.

'Knobheads,' says Bartels, leaning back.

Kringe looks at him and then the rest of us. 'Massive arseholes,' he says. 'I'm telling you guys.'

Brux stands up and says to me: 'We'll keep in touch by phone, Ms Riley.' He says it in a very engaging way. He says it like he takes me seriously. His eyes are completely open and clear.

'Yes,' I say. 'We'll talk.'

'I'll show you out,' says Tschauner.

We stand up and leave.

We walk together down the corridor to the lift.

On the wall outside an open-plan office is a postcard from Istanbul. I stare at it a fraction too long.

'From Inceman,' says Tschauner. 'He sent it at the beginning of last week. He was here for a long time before he went to homicide. You worked with him once, didn't you? Do you remember?'

Oh yes, I remember. Although I'd be the last person he'd send a postcard to.

'How is he?' I ask.

'Hang on a moment.' Tschauner pulls the card from the wall. 'Hmm: *"Dear Former Colleagues, Yesterday there was a big drugs bust in the restaurant round the corner, which reminded me of you. I'm doing fairly OK, sometimes I even forget that I've only got one arm. Put it this way – the wound is healing. I might open a hotel with an old friend soon, then you can all come and visit. Best wishes from the Bosporus, Bülent."* So even now you don't know exactly how he is, do you? Weren't you there when he lost his arm?'

I goggle at Tschauner as if I'd just been sent a gruesome message from the other side.

And it is a bit like that.

There's nothing colder than dead love.

I say 'Hmm' and 'See you' and stride away, and don't look round as the little scrap of card in Tschauner's hand shoots bolts of red lightning at my back.

At home, I chuck my bag onto the bed, have a second shower and a fourth coffee and then sit down at the window. Ponder. Try to sort things out. There's the Austrian in hospital. Faller appears next to him.

There are the drugs in the east. The Albanian appears next to them.

And there's that Faller again.

There's Calabretta, who suddenly seems like a stranger to me.

There's Klatsche, who presses me up against cellar walls at night, and I like it. And his ex-colleagues smashed the Austrian's bones to smithereens.

And then from right offstage, Inceman grabs me round the heart.

I should be drinking beer not coffee, but I had enough of that yesterday.

Something's ringing.

My phone.

Carla.

At least that's unambiguous – friendship.

'Hey,' I say. 'What's up?'

'That's what I was about to ask you,' she says.

'Why?'

'Klatsche,' she says. 'Has he got something going on? Kiez-wise, I mean?'

'Apart from his bar, you mean?'

'Apart from his bar,' she says.

'Not that I know of,' I say.

As if I could be the one who ought to know if he had anything like that on. I ought to lock him up right away if he's got anything on. Strictly speaking.

'Why do you ask?'

A foghorn, and Carla breathing out. She's standing outside her café door, smoking.

'Oh, I don't know myself,' she says. 'He just came round and went straight in to Rocco in the kitchen and asked him something. I wasn't listening, wasn't interested. But there was suddenly something in the air between them. And then I did listen.'

'And?'

'Rocco was more or less shouting at Klatsche that he wanted nothing to do with that shit. That he wanted "abso-bloody-lutely nothing to do with that shit". End quote.'

'Do you have any idea what shit it could be?' I ask.

'No-oo,' she says. 'Rocco didn't want to talk about it. He said it wasn't important. But he doesn't shout if it isn't important, you know?'

'Uh-huh.'

'You could have a word with Klatsche if you get a chance. Stop him getting into trouble.'

Seems like a few of the men around me have a good chance of getting themselves into trouble.

'I'll see if he'll talk to me,' I say. 'Thanks for the tip-off.'

'Hey, no worries,' she says. I can hear her smoking again.

'Shall we go for a beer?' I ask.

'What's the time?'

'Half past four,' I say.

'That's beer o'clock, isn't it?'

'That's definitely beer o'clock,' I say. 'Shall I come to you?'

'Don't worry,' she says. 'I'll come to you. See you in half an hour outside the snack bar on your road. The kitchen's closed here anyway; the lunchtime crowd ate everything. And Rocco can manage drinks and stuff on his own. I'll just pull my apron off and head over.'

Click.

OK.

It's cold but that doesn't matter.

The wooden bench in front of the kiosk.

Coat buttoned up, collar turned up, beer bottles open.

Like summer, only colder.

'Hair of the dog,' I say, and we clink bottles.

'A few beers yesterday, huh?'

I nod. 'I had to go east. For work.'

'And you drank so much you need the hair of the dog today? Must have been a great job.'

'Let's not talk about it, OK?'

'That's the second time I've heard that today.'

'Sorry. But it's so complicated.'

She nods.

It's OK.

As we drink, we watch the street doing its thing.

Cars.

Bikes.

Bicycle courier.

People holding coffee cups.

People holding beer bottles.

People holding children.

Then I fetch another two beers.

Then we drink.

Then Carla fetches another two beers.

Then I tell her about Inceman.

About his postcard.

Which wasn't even for me, but which got to me anyway.

She says she understands.

That it's getting me down, that is.

She says perhaps I should fly out to Istanbul and talk to him.

I tell her that's not an option.

Firstly, there's nothing to talk about.

Secondly, he doesn't want to talk to me.

If I had a new arm for him, then yeah.

But I haven't.

And thirdly, because of Klatsche.

I couldn't do a thing like that.

We've got to the point where I can't just fly off to another man even though I'd rather end up in bed with him than be anywhere else.

Can I?

I fetch another two beers.

Once all the beer's all gone, it's half past seven.

'I think I'll get some sleep,' I say.

Carla nods.

'You do that, love.'

We stand up and hug, a long second longer than grown women normally do.

We always do that.

It's been a lovely evening.

I wake up because he creeps up on me from behind, takes me in his arms, kisses the back of my neck. Note to self: he wants something. He can have it. I keep my eyes shut, and it's all hands, hands, hands, and all skin, skin, skin, and his stubble everywhere, and his hair, and he smells so amazing, smells of pub, and eau-de-pub always makes me forgetful.

Later on, the sky is full of clouds; there's no moon and no light, because the only streetlamp outside our building has been broken for ages; we lie side by side and we're just the gleam of two glowing cigarettes.

'Are you OK?' I ask.

He doesn't answer, just puffs on his cigarette.

After a while: 'Why do you ask?'

'No reason.'

He stubs out his cigarette, turns over and pretends to be asleep.

St Georg Hospital, sometime between yesterday and today.

'So, let's see what I've brought us … Newspapers, beer, cigarettes … We can really settle in for a while, Joe.'

'What would I do without you, Faller?'

'Oh, you'd have someone else.'

'Who, then?'

'Santa, maybe.'

'You look like him.'

'Really?'

'No, Faller, you look miles better than Santa.'

'Do you want to go out and smoke?'

'Let's have a beer and read the papers first. And turn the telly off, if you don't mind. That guy gets on my nerves.'

'If you had a gun, you could just shoot it off.'

'I could. But I don't have a gun.'

'Would you if you did?'

'Depends.'

'On what?'

'Various things.'

'Money?'

'Not necessarily.'

'What then?'

'If he deserved it. Don't forget: that's not actually my job any more.'

'True. It's more of a hobby for you.'

'Yes, it's more of a hobby for me, Faller.'

'Must be fun.'

'I wouldn't call it that. It's more … satisfying.'

'There needs to be a point to it?'

'Exactly. There needs to be a point to it. What about you?'
'I can't knock anyone off, Joe.'
'Are you sure?'
'I am now.'
'What does that mean?'
'Long story.'
'Tell me.'
'No.'
'No?'
'No.'
'OK.'
'Shall I open the beer?'
'Yeah, sure.'

Two men, two bottles of beer.
   No paper.
   Silence.

'Faller?'
   'Yes?'
   'Can I ask you a girly question?'
   'What would that be?'
   'What are you thinking about?'
   'That is a damn girly question.'
   'I know. So?'
   'I'm thinking that there could be a simple solution to a compli-
cated question – a solution that is right there between us, staring up
at me from your hospital bedside table.'
   'And how does that go?'
   'The hitman in me is the hitman in you, Joe.'
   'Interesting approach.'

DROSTE, PAUL

Now you have to stay cool of course.

Someone tried to hit me up in the street.

For meth.

Might be coincidence. But might mean the word's out.

In which case he knows. And we're dead.

ADELMANN, NICO

The first thing to do is not panic. Just calmly shag your old lady. True thing. You don't want to freak out. Just because somebody said something.

Drob reckons the boss knows the stunt we're pulling.

I reckon that's bollocks and I'm totally confident about that.

NIEHUS, ROBERT

The thing now is to make sure the delivery runs as fucking smooth as it did last time.

Then we grab the stuff and vanish.

Worst-case scenario, I mean.

MALAJ, GJERGJ

Unbelievable.

First my cousins are all too stupid to take my place, or too weak or too dumb or too vain or too crazy.

And then three little punks try to screw me over.

It's time.

GOOD WITH THE OTHER PERSON'S BAD MOOD

And as I'm on the way to the hospital to ask Austrian Ski-Teacher-Hitman Joe who the hell he thinks he is, I meet Faller outside the main entrance.

'Oh no,' I say.

'Yes,' he says.

'Have you got a new best friend, Faller?'

It's just after ten. Faller must have got up really early to visit Joe. Maybe he hoped it would be early enough not to bump into me.

He looks at me with a kind of puppy-dog stare and breathes deeply in and out. Then he takes my hand, leads me to a bench and we sit down.

'We should talk, my girl.'

'I think so too.'

He looks up to the gloomy sky and says: 'It's like this…'

'It's like this: I'm the idiot in this story,' I say.

'No you're not.'

'Yes I am. I spend days talking to this stupid mystery-monger till I'm blue in the face; I sit at his bedside, I hold his hand, I bring him beer, I bring him cigarettes, I bring him food. I even properly like him, and I get the feeling he likes me too. And what does he do? Sends me off on a treasure hunt in the east so that you can just turn up and he can have all the time in the world to tell you everything important. That's what it looks like, doesn't it?'

'I know it must look like that to you, Chas.'

What else should it look like?

'But I don't know any more than you. I probably just know

different things. And it would definitely be a good idea for us to pool our information instead of digging up the hatchet. We know quite a lot between us, I reckon.'

'What do you know, then?' I ask.

'Well, I don't know his real name, for example; but I didn't ask, because it doesn't matter,' says Faller. 'I know that he spent decades bumping people off.'

'I know that too, now, you joker. Do you know what type of people they were?'

'People who picked the wrong guys in the Kiez to mess with. Dealers, pimps, blackmailers, protection money collectors ... No women, no kids. Or so he says.'

'Old school, huh?'

'Basically.'

'And who was he working for?' I ask.

'Here's where it gets exciting,' says Faller.

'Malaj, wasn't it?'

'How do you know that?'

'It's the impression I brought back from the east,' I say.

Faller nods and sits brooding. Then he says: 'But.'

'But what?'

'Interestingly, the Albanian gradually pulled him out of the hitman work. Before Joe met him, he did jobs for all kinds of Kiez bosses, but wasn't closely linked to any of them. The classic phantom. Made him very successful. I kept hearing about him too, but only as a rumour. Nobody who spoke about him had ever even met him.'

He pulls his Roth-Händle out of his coat pocket, lights a cigarette for himself and holds the packet out to me.

'Thanks,' I say, 'I've got my own.'

'What are those Indian pipes?' he asks when he sees my packet.

'I brought them home from the east too,' I say.

'Must have been a hell of a time over there,' he says.

'Keep going,' I say, 'and then I'll tell you something in return.'

'OK.' He takes a breath. 'Gjergj Malaj obviously realised that a phantom like Joe could be very useful to him. And he hired him to be exactly that. Someone who could suddenly turn up any time, anywhere; someone potentially deadly – everyone knows that. He made him into his mysterious long arm.'

We puff on our cigarettes.

'When was that?' I ask.

'That was at exactly the same time that Malaj himself was getting out of all his red-light businesses and only investing in property. Around the millennium. But via Joe, he was always there in the background. And because everyone knew that, nobody did any deals that might damage the Albanian.'

'Because everyone knew that except us,' I say.

'We hadn't the least idea that there was anyone like Joe,' says Faller.

'Did he kill at all for the Albanian?'

'Twice.'

I drag on my cigarette. 'Why did he tell you all this?'

Faller shrugs. 'Perhaps he wants to wipe the slate clean.'

'You mean that he'll turn supergrass?' I ask. 'So he can start a new life in the Austrian Alps?'

Faller looks at me with unusually big eyes for an old bumblebee like him, and the eyes say: What else?

'Please,' I say. 'That stuff only happens in mafia fairy tales. It's a gangster myth. If a guy who's spent half his life shooting people down spills the beans like that, there's a better reason behind it than just looking for peace. And how do we know everything he told you is true?'

'We don't, of course. But there'll be some truth in it. The story makes sense; it goes some way towards explaining why, in all those years when the Albanian was supposedly off the scene, nobody tried to become the new king.'

'Or why nobody succeeded.'

Faller shrugs. 'So what do you know?' he asks.

'That Joe's an unofficial grass for the drugs squad in Saxony. Or for one particular narcotics officer, to be precise. I don't think his colleagues know about it. Because hiring an ex-hitman isn't really the done thing.'

'Oh,' says Faller. 'What's the done thing and what's done are often two very different kettles of fish … Joe said he'd practically sent you to Leipzig.'

'He did. He wanted me to talk to a man named Wieczorkowski about crocodiles.'

Faller looks confused, but the corners of his mouth twitch in amusement.

'Yeah, I looked like that too,' I say. 'But then, when I got there and talked to Wieczorkowski, I realised that it's anything but funny.'

'Wieczorkowski is the narc you mentioned just now?'

I nod.

'Why did he take Joe on as a source? How did they meet?'

'He didn't want to tell me,' I say. 'According to him, the chance was there and he took it. About two weeks ago, Joe told him there was a big meth deal in the pipeline between Hamburg and the Czech Republic.'

'Oh. That's bad.'

'Yep. But meth is nothing compared to krok. A cheap Russian drug. Made from codeine, formic acid and match heads. And it eats you alive.'

'It eats you alive?'

I tell him what Wieczorkowski told me. And what I saw in Leipzig.

'I'm not following, Chas. What's connected to what? I thought this was about meth?'

'It is. Or the big deal is. How krokodil fits in, only Joe knows. But it must have something to do with it, or he wouldn't have mentioned it.'

'Are you on your way to ask him?'

'I'm on my way to ask him,' I say, standing up and stubbing my cigarette out on the bin.

'OK,' says Faller, staying seated.

'OK,' I say.

'See you,' he says.

'See you.'

Just before the door closes behind me, I turn round and see Faller still sitting there.

I don't exactly know why I didn't tell him about Drob, Adlo and Ronny, but I had the feeling that he was keeping something back and that I should do the same.

I'm starting to feel like this is all a game of chess, and we're just pieces that someone else is pushing around the board.

Faller has a particular look on his face.

Like he's found a secret door to a room stuffed full of splendid things that belong to him alone.

Joe is sitting cheerfully in his bed.

'There you are again,' he says.

'There you are still,' I say.

'Where would I go without you?'

'You can stick your charm.'

I pull up a chair and sit down.

'Wieczorkowski thought you might be dead.'

'He was worried about me?'

'Not exactly,' I say. 'I think he was more afraid for his delicate plan.'

He hints at a smile. 'What else? How was East Germany?'

'I learnt a lot,' I say. 'That you're a hitman, for example, and that you work for one of the most dangerous men in Hamburg...'

'Worked...' he says.

'Can I believe that?'

'Nothing I tell you is a lie.'

I look into his eyes.

He looks into my eyes.

I would like to believe him.

'What else does Wieczorkowski say, apart from he's glad I'm alive?'

'He's wondering what's up with the drugs deal you told him about. And what krokodil has to do with it. And I'm wondering that too.'

'So many questions,' he says, sucking his teeth.

'Shall we go for a smoke?' I ask.

'I've been for a smoke already today. Can you come back this afternoon?'

'Ask Faller. I'm sure he'd like to come.'

That sounds a bit hurt, but hey.

'Are you jealous?'

'Maybe,' I say.

'Nice of you to be so honest.'

He moves his head to and fro, stretching his neck muscles as if he were a boxer. It doesn't seem to hurt any more. He seems to have got a lot more mobile in general in the last few days. At least round the neck.

'So,' he says. 'I also told you about those guys.'

'Drob, Adlo and Ronny?'

He nods. 'They want to use the crystal deal for a deal of their own. For krok.'

'You said that already. How exactly is that meant to work?'

'I don't know. I only know that they'll seriously piss off the big guy. And that they shouldn't do that.'

'Does the big guy know?' I ask.

'The little shits took me out of action before I could tell him about their plan,' he says. 'But he wouldn't be him if he didn't know already.'

Joe lifts his splinted arm, probably doing a few little exercises. He can already do so much. Soon he'll be hopping from the bed to the wheelchair all by himself.

'They found out that you wanted to tip him off?' I ask.

'They smelt it,' he says. 'Rats smell that stuff. But they only found out that *I'd* found something out. It was meant to be my elegant exit, you know. Employee of the month one last time and then get out of the whole mob.'

'As easy as that?'

'Well, we'd have seen about that. I'm good at disappearing, though. One of my key skills, you might say.'

'Has Gjergj Malaj tried to contact you?' I ask. 'He must know you're here.'

'He hasn't visited yet.'

'There's a policeman outside your door,' I say.

He looks at me. 'You've only just spotted that?'

Of course. If Gjergj Malaj wants to get in here, he won't shy away from a single policeman on guard duty.

He looks at me thoughtfully.

'Do you think he wants you dead?'

'I've got life insurance, remember?'

'Does that nettle him?'

'Oh yes,' he says. 'That nettles him.'

But he seems unsettled all the same.

'You have to stop it,' he says, and for a brief moment he looks miles away.

'I can't station a whole century outside your door,' I say.

'Not my death,' he says, irritated. 'I mean the krok. And maybe you could shoot the meth deal down too. That shit doesn't kill people as fast as krokodil, but it turns them into zombies.'

Strange to hear this from someone like him. But I sense that he means it.

There seems to have been a change in him over the last two days.

He's got a Faller at his side now, and a Faller can make you feel a peculiar need for justice. I'd forgotten that, but now it's coming back to me.

'It takes over from everything you love, right?'

'Right,' he says. 'It takes over from everything you love.'

'Help us,' I say.

'I've told you all I know.'

'Testify against Malaj.'

He looks at me like I've asked him to take out the US president.

'If you'll shoot me right afterwards, we can talk about it.'

'I thought we might be able to talk about a state's evidence thing,' I say. 'Faller thinks so too, by the way.'

I'm trying everything now.

'That's bullshit,' he says. 'The very idea…' He laughs somewhat manically and shakes his head.

'So why are you telling me so much about Malaj?' I ask.

'I'm not telling you anything. I'm tossing you crumbs from which you can make your own loaf, if you're clever enough. And you were the one who suddenly starting throwing that name around.' He looks at me, and there's something painful in his eyes. 'You know what? I just want to go home.'

'Where do you live? I'll drive you.'

'I don't want to go to some flat,' he says. 'I want to go back to the mountains. I want to live in the Alps again and maybe be a normal human being for a few years. But before you leave a place where you've lived well for a long time, you tidy up a bit. That's how it should be, isn't it?'

'That's what this is about? You want to ease your conscience?'

'I can't do that,' he says. 'I don't have to. I left my conscience in the cloakroom a lifetime ago. But now things have turned out like this – me here, and you too, both of us in this weird place, the others and all their shit … You have to take life as it comes. And if I can stop a few arseholes from poisoning a bunch of kids, then I will. I don't have to shop anyone. I just have to get people like you to look in the right corners.'

'And if Malaj finds you? Maybe not here, but in your sodding mountains? You can't even climb.'

'I used to be able to climb like a chamois,' he says, 'believe it or not.'

'The main thing is whether you believe it.'

When I come out of the front door, Faller's gone.

I was expecting him to wait for me.

*

I wasn't expecting Brux to want me in on anything. But it seems he does, and so here I am sitting in the car with Kringe and Bartels, driving in pursuit of Ronny. Eventually, after we'd spent hours hanging around outside his flat in Altona, he came out. A nervous, skinny little man in a dark-blue bomber jacket, which is both too baggy and too short. His blonde hair is pretty thin, but he hasn't even noticed, let alone accepted it. Apart from that: grey cowboy boots and jeans with white writing on the bum.

Now he's sitting in an old copper-coloured Golf, heading south on the A7.

With us behind him.

'Where's he off to now?' Kringe moans into his blonde three-day stubble.

Bartels mutters.

Kringe drives.

'Container port,' I say as Ronny's Golf turns off the motorway at Waltershof.

This time Kringe mutters and Bartels says: 'It's high tide. That's when the big tubs come in. And the big things come on the big tubs. Maybe he's got something to pick up.'

'Or something to check out,' says Kringe.

'You won't even get close to them,' I say.

'Close to what?'

'The big tubs. The terminals are sealed off.'

'Not if you know someone who'll wave you through,' says Bartels.

Now it's my turn to mutter, because at that precise moment I think: all these lanes are confusing as hell – you could take the wrong one in nothing flat and then you'd be right out of it.

And as I think that, Kringe says: 'Bloody hell!'

And Bartels shouts: 'I don't believe it!'

Kringe slams his foot down hard, for all the good that'll do – we're just in time to wave to the left rear mudguard on Ronny's Golf before he vanishes: he's nipped very smartly and very suddenly over into the filter lane and dived into a tunnel in the maze of streets on our right.

We sail serenely on.

Like absolute bloody beginners.

It doesn't matter a damn whether he noticed us, if we just cocked up or both. The fish has slipped the hook.

We trawl around the port a bit and keep an eye out for that stupid copper-coloured Golf; our attempts are not, naturally, crowned with success. We drink sour coffee at a snack bar and smoke a few bitter cigarettes, and we all show an astonishing ability to put up with each other's bad moods.

Behind us and in front of us and to the sides of us, cranes nod in the wind.

I think they're laughing at us.

Around one in the morning, my phone rings. I was about to go to bed.

I don't know the number.

'Hello?'

'Brux here.'

'Mr Brux, what's up?'

'Listen, we've had a tip-off: there's about to be a raid on Lincolnstrasse – Graciosa Bar. Tschauner says you live nearby. We'd like to have you there. Shall we pick you up?'

'I don't know. It's not even my department.'

'It is now.'

'Who says so?'

'Dr Kolb. The new attorney general.'

'I've heard of her,' I say.

'There, you see. And she's heard of you.'

'I don't quite understand.'

'Kolb wants you to take over.'

'OK,' I say, and my heart would leap if it dared. 'I'll be outside my door in seven minutes.'

'All right, we'll be downstairs.'

Mad.

I scramble back into my clothes so fast it would make even the fire brigade dizzy.

As I hurry down the stairs five minutes later, my colleagues are already in the middle of the road, engine running.

I might not know exactly what game I'm in – but I'm back in.

There's tinsel lametta hanging from the ceiling. Wonky faces are glued to the bar. The rest are dancing on the tables, legs and arms in the air, electronic music in their ears and in their bellies. There aren't many tables, it's a small place. Like the door off the staircase. We had to squeeze through it. But that makes it easy to secure. Brux has stationed four officers in front of it. That should be plenty.

My colleagues wave their IDs in the air and it all goes pretty fast after that. Lights on, music off, party over.

Stored in a cellar behind the bar are three kilos of uncut crystal meth, packed in ten-gram portions.

Official spoils: a Hamburg market value of a good three hundred thousand euros.

One: the biggest haul that's ever turned up here.

Two: now they've clocked that we've clocked them.

Three: there were no crocodiles there.

Meanwhile, on the other side of the night.

DROSTE, PAUL

Ronny reckons the fuzz were on his tail today. He says they followed him, maybe even from his house. But he didn't notice till they got to the port. Then he got out of there. Shook them off. The fuzz. So he says.

That's always the thing with Ronny. What he says. And what's true.

Let's hope he did shake them off.

And then there's all the fuss with the boss.

We've parked the gear for now and we're going underground.

Shit, huh?

ADELMANN, NICO

Hello? We're all tense. But Drob's really making waves, and it's really pissing me off.

Doesn't trust Ronny any more. Or me, I don't think.

Wants us to hide. Wants to go into hiding himself until all the deliveries are done.

I mean: hey, if it all works out, the deliveries will last YEARS. You have to relax a bit at some time, don't you?

I told my girl yesterday, C'mon baby, pick out something nice for yourself. Start with some pretty dresses and stop with a little place in the country.

Course, she keeps asking where I'm going to earn so much money.

I say nothing. I lay her in bed and work my magic on her. It makes her forget all her questions.

NIEHUS, ROBERT

Wimps. Both of them.

I know how it is in the big time. They have no idea. Two, three deliveries I'll do with them. Then they're out. Then I'll take over the big league.

They're driving me crazy. One's all pathetic panic and the other's all over-the-top relaxed.

I've already got a new partner. From Sarajevo.

Badass guy. Just my type.

We'll really set up shop and wipe the floor with the rest of them. Even the old guys will have to get that it's over. You just have to look at them: they're full.

I won't hide. I'm hungry.

MALAJ, GJERGJ

Give Gaetano credit for one thing: his boys could be done for speeding.

Little joke.

JOE

You don't need much to make contact with the outside. You just need a good carrier pigeon.

FALLER, GEORG

This is how I see it: if I talk about the one thing, I must be able to talk about the others too.

Mustn't I?

AS IF SOMEONE HAD PLANTED A BOMB AMONG US

Klatsche calls while I'm on my way to the office, just as I'm tramping through the park. I'm tired from last night, there are a couple of gulls shrieking above my head and a gaggle of geese cackle in the meadow to my left, probably discussing their next formation flight.

'Hey,' I say.

'Hey.' He sounds strained and I can already hear a heap of trouble in his voice.

'What's happened?'

'I need your help.'

It's the first time since we met that Klatsche's needed my help. Usually, I need his.

'Can you come to the Blue Night?'

'What's up?'

'There are three dead men lying in my cellar.'

'Oh.'

Three dead men. Obviously, it's a message.

'I don't know what to do, Chas, I…'

'Have you touched anything?'

'No, fuck's sake, shit … Please just come.'

I turn on my heel, flag down a taxi on Millerntorplatz and say: 'Hang in there. I'll be with you in five minutes.'

It's only a short ride, just down the Reeperbahn. At Hans-Albers-Platz I press five euros into the driver's hand and jump out.

There's no wind and a deep, damp sky is hanging over the city.

There's hardly anyone about on the Sinful Mile. Just a few stragglers from last night, young people totally off their heads.

There are mountains of rubbish and broken bottles lying on the square. It stinks of beer and God knows what. Some of the neon signs are on, a grubby light here, a faint blinking there. The squinting, blurry lights of the Kiez in the morning. As if the houses are still half asleep. Of course nobody can see properly with bleary panda eyes like that.

Klatsche's standing outside his bar. He looks as though he's been smoking non-stop for at least half an hour. There are little beads of sweat on his upper lip, his hands are trembling; this beanpole looks thinner than ever. His hair's stopped standing on end. Klatsche's had a shock.

'Hey,' I say.

He stands facing me, his left arm pointing downwards, tensed at his side, and his right hand gripping it; every few seconds, the hand frees itself and gives the mouth a drag on the cigarette they're sharing, then everything clamps back together again. He's swaying ever so slightly to and fro.

I'd like to take him in my arms, but his posture is screaming 'Please Don't Touch'.

'OK,' I say quietly. 'You just stand here and wait for me. I'll go down and have a look.'

The hand with the cigarette goes to the mouth again and I think he nods.

The door to the Blue Night is ajar; I go in. That silence when nobody's there, but it's crystal clear that something is, and it's nothing good. I know that silence. Its presence means that something murderous has paid a visit. The very first time I experienced that silence was when I found my dad with his head on the desk, and actually that was once too many. This silence is like a shock edging through the room, freezing everything it touches.

Every step is an effort. Like in those dreams where you're trying to get somewhere, but your feet seem to have been welded to the floor.

Eventually, I'm standing behind the bar.

The hatch to the cellar, to our cellar, is open. I climb carefully down the steps, trying not to touch anything, even though that's nonsense. There are traces of me everywhere down here, I had sex against the wall a couple of nights ago.

I can't find the damn light switch. Phone out, torch mode on.

Lying right in front of me are three corpses.

I almost stumble over them.

They're all lying face down, hands secured behind their backs with white cable ties and, as far as I can tell, each of these gentleman has a massive hole in his head; it's a hell of a mess at any rate. The guy in the middle is wearing a dark-blue bomber jacket, grey cowboy boots and jeans with white writing on the bum.

I guess that's Ronny, who slipped through our fingers yesterday at the port and, presumably, whose meth we pinched last night.

OK. In that case, I can figure out who the other two are.

I climb carefully back up again, leave the cellar hatch as it is and light a cigarette for myself outside with Klatsche.

'How did Drob, Adlo and Ronny land up in your cellar?'

He inhales smoke, and exhales again, and says: 'I let them in. Because apparently I'm a complete idiot.'

I raise my eyebrows and look at him. I'm aiming for stern, but I don't know whether I've pulled it off, or whether it's appropriate.

'They came round a couple of days ago,' he says. 'Asked if they could park something here.'

'Park what exactly?'

'I don't know. I didn't ask, and I said no right away. It was too hot for me.'

'And then you asked Rocco if they could park it with him.'

'How do you know that?' He gives me a distraught look.

'Never mind.' I wave it away.

'There's no harm in asking,' he says. 'And I felt like I owed them something, you know? I'm doing so well, I'm out of that shit. So sometimes when I'm around old colleagues who're still involved, I get a kind of … oh, I don't know … kind of … I want to mother them.'

'You grab on to any responsibility you come across,' I say.

'Only with people who're stuck in the shit!' he says, wagging his left index finger in the air.

So obviously that makes me ask why *I* always get the feeling that he'd like to take on more responsibility when it comes to us. Are we in the shit?

Or is it just me?

'Yesterday evening, the lads came to my place again,' he says, 'and suddenly they wanted to park themselves. They wanted to hide, were scared stiff of something – no idea what. Course, I thought: better keep out, there'll be some nasty reason why they need to keep out of the firing line for a few hours. But I couldn't leave them out in the rain either.' He drags on his cigarette. 'I told them they could hide in my cellar if they absolutely had to. But to bugger off again by morning. The door from the cellar to the yard is only bolted on the inside so they could have got out any time.'

'But clearly they couldn't,' I say. 'How did the others get into your cellar then?'

'They must have picked the lock on my steel door,' he says, pointing to the entrance. 'There's not really anything to see. It's done as neatly as if they had a key. I couldn't have done it, and I can do a bit with doors, as you know.'

He looks at me and, yeah, I reckon he's about to cry.

'Oh shit, Chas, I've fucked up. And it didn't even do the boys any good.'

'I don't think you could have saved them,' I say. 'They were in such deep trouble they'd have been killed anyway. We just need to be careful that nothing else goes wrong here.'

'Meaning?'

'Cards on the table. We call Calabretta.'

He lights another cigarette; down on the Reeperbahn, a groaning group of males staggers past – a wretched bridegroom and his mates, I reckon.

Klatsche draws deeply on his cigarette and eyes up the drunken lads for a few seconds.

'Perhaps I don't even know how the three of them got into my cellar?'

'Not a good idea,' I say. 'If even one person saw you talking to them here, you'd be in all kinds of shit.'

'But perhaps Calabretta could…?'

'Klatsche?'

'Yes?'

'He can't and he won't.'

He lets his shoulders sag along with his head and the cigarette.

I lay my hand on his cheek. 'Don't worry. You didn't do anything, apart from open up your cellar for a few old friends. You don't have anything to do with those guys any more, do you?'

He shakes his head, but it looks a bit as though he doesn't even really know himself.

'I'll call him now, OK?'

He nods and says: 'Well, I'll smoke a few more cigarettes then.'

It's nuts watching Calabretta take down Klatsche's personal details. Although I'm standing between the two of them, it's really more like I'm standing next to Klatsche. I think it's more comfortable for all of us that way.

Klatsche gives an amazingly clear explanation of what happened. I get the impression he's pulling himself together again. And as he tells the story and I listen, I realise that basically everything's fine. It's quite obvious that the boy's above suspicion.

'So,' says Calabretta once he's taken the statement, 'we ought to go to the records department to get your fingerprints done.' He tacks on: 'Just to compare them with any prints left by the culprits.'

'No need,' says Klatsche.

Calabretta looks puzzled. Then light dawns. 'True. We've got them already.'

'Yeah,' says Klatsche. 'You ought to still have them from before.'

It's not easy for him to say that. He's always so proud of having made it out of that scene.

'What about me?' I ask. I feel the need for a clear declaration of solidarity. 'I've had my fingers all over the place too.'

Both men look at me and I know: one sees it one way, and the other another.

'Shall we go round the corner to the Davidwache station?'

'We can do,' says Calabretta and nods, and then Brückner and Schulle drive up and get out of their patrol car and look important, and I'm still caught in no-man's land, and I definitely feel like I'm in the wrong film.

If it was all a bit funnier, I'd be laughing.

Klatsche's gone down to his pub. That sounds a bit like: gone down with his ship. It's not quite like that, but his face looked pretty sick, like he'd really come through something. I reckon he thinks that's it for a proper life. He thinks that after that stunt the only options open to him are the wrong ones. So in a way something did go down with the ship. Fucked up. Even though Calabretta told him not to worry as he said goodbye. And Schulle and Brückner stood beside him and kept slapping him on the shoulders and smoking cigarettes with him and saying they wouldn't leave till their forensics colleagues had gone too.

Then I was allowed to hug him.

All the same, everything gives him the creeps now.

Now I'm sitting with Calabretta in a room right at the back of the Davidwache that is actually sort of like an interview room. There's a table and four chairs and a little window with bars outside it.

Left my fingerprints and my DNA behind.

I'm feeling kind of itchy – not massively, but a bit.

'That's perfectly normal,' he says.

We both know that nothing's normal this morning yet everything's the same as ever.

'In the broadest terms, that was Gjergj Malaj,' I say, trying to wipe the black ink off my fingertips with a damp paper towel.

'The lads in Klatsche's cellar?'

Inspector Calabretta pulls an irritated face and wets a couple more paper towels for me in the washbasin in the far corner of the room.

'Why do you say that? Because in the end he's always been behind everything in this city? Or because executions like that are just his style?'

He sits down again.

I keep working on my hands and tell him about Wieczorkowski's theory. About Hamburg being lined up as the trading centre for meth in Western Europe. And that there's really only ever been one person who could get something like that up and running in this town.

'I also know that those three were involved in a big drugs deal,' I say. 'They were probably meant to arrange things, prepare the ground. And then they must have thought they could get away with branching out a bit. There was that bust yesterday where we found three kilos of meth. I can't imagine that Malaj would hide his stuff that amateurishly…'

I hold my right hand up to the light. It looks quite presentable again.

Calabretta drums his fingers on the table top. 'Where did the tip-off for the raid come from?'

'Anonymous, according to Brux and his guys. Probably a source they want to keep below the radar.'

'That would be an interesting person to meet then,' says Calabretta.

'It would,' I say. 'But I think our colleagues in drugs would be pretty stubborn. They're almost as careful as customs. Which is understandable.'

Now my left hand.

'In any case, I'm pretty sure that the three dealers died over the meth we found in the raid.'

'Then we can also start by assuming that the crystal really belonged to the big boss and that the three minnows wanted to indulge in an extra bonus for themselves,' says Calabretta. 'And keep that going for quite a while.'

'It's pure speculation, of course,' I say, 'but you could think along those lines. And, yes, I think we should.'

'OK. Join forces, huh?'

'Definitely. I'll speak to Dr Kolb,' I say, 'and we'll all sit round one big table by this afternoon at the latest.'

'Dr Kolb...' says Calabretta. 'She's the new attorney general...?'

'Exactly. Last night, for unaccountable reasons, she let me swap hats and go out with the drugs boys. As for the ex-hitman in the hospital, I've more or less hung up that hat...'

'Ex-hitman?'

'The guy in the St Georg hospital. I told you about him, didn't I?'

He nods.

'He was a professional killer in the Kiez.'

'No way.'

'Way,' I say. 'And he's also an unofficial source for the drugs team in Saxony and has been on good terms with Gjergj Malaj for years.'

Calabretta shakes his head as if someone has slapped him.

'He's a walking, talking contradiction,' I say, lobbing a pile of damp tissues into the bin. My left hand still has a load of black on it, but that's OK. It's supporting Klatsche. 'We'll all roll up to the HQ and then take our time to piece things together.'

'OK,' he says, standing up and smoothing out his leather jacket. 'Let's go.'

Yes.

Let's go.

Inspector Calabretta's unshakable pragmatism has become part of the bedrock of my life.

'How are you doing?' I ask once we've left the Davidwache and are on our way to his car, which he's parked *carabiniere*-style right outside the door. 'About Betty, I mean.'

'Betty? Betty who?'

He opens the passenger door for me. The blue 'Police' sign shines out into the dull morning from the redbrick façade behind his head.

'Just another crick in my heart,' he says, walking round his car and getting in on the driver's side.

Like I always say – hunting criminals isn't the cure for everything, but it sure helps with all kinds of stuff.

We drive north in the Alfa. Calabretta summons his team together and I phone Dr Kolb, who is happy to nod through my attendance for a second time.

Something's clanking in the front of the car.

So here we are again. Schulle, Brückner, Calabretta, Brux, Tschauner, Kringe and Bartels. All round one big table. Only Inceman is missing.

I'm not the only one to notice.

'We just need our man in Istanbul,' says Schulle.

We all have to bear a moment's pain. But I need to push it away. I can't deal with it so well.

So I write on the big white wall with a firm hand and a black pen, listing everything we know, just like everything's fine, and then I use a blue pen to add everything we suspect. Brux and Calabretta stick a few photos up too. There's no photo of Joe – officially he hasn't got a role to play. I try to keep him hidden as far as possible. I don't know why, but I feel like I owe him that.

We end up with a picture like this:

Gjergj Malaj wants to make the Port of Hamburg into the crystal-meth hub for Western Europe. That would be a low-risk, long-term, highly profitable spring, gushing with money that could be laundered via his property business in Hamburg, or his hotels and casinos in Prague. Drob, Adlo and Ronny stupidly tried to muscle in on it in some way, and now they're dead.

It goes without saying that we won't be able to pin the murders on him. He wouldn't be Malaj if he's made any silly mistakes. A couple of pros did it for him and if we catch them, we'd be awesome, because they will have left the country a long time ago.

But we can fuck up his drugs business.

And we need to find out about the krok Joe mentioned.

'What we need is a concrete statement from your informant,' says Brux.

'I'll head straight there,' I say, 'but don't hold your breath.'

'It's important to have an in-depth dialogue with Leipzig and Prague too,' says Calabretta.

'I'll discuss it with Wieczorkowski,' says Brux. 'Not a problem.'

Just at that moment, my phone rings, and it's Wieczorkowski on the line and at the table.

'Fancy that,' I say. 'We were just talking about you. How are you?'

'I think I'm on my way to Hamburg.'

'You think you're on your way to Hamburg? How come?'

'I was hanging around the Vietnamese markets for a bit this morning…'

The line crackles and crunches and slurs. He's in the car. The phone network is still very patchy out east.

'In your highly inconspicuous Ford Transit?' I ask.

'I was travelling on foot,' he says. 'The Transit waited patiently in the forest.'

Of course the Indian talks about his car like it's a horse.

'Let's talk turkey,' he says and his voice keeps chuckling like it chuckled the first time we spoke on the phone.

'Great,' I say. 'We love turkey.'

'OK,' he says, 'listen up. Suddenly there was this lorry. Hamburg plates, a haulier based in the container port. The driver stopped at the market for a coffee while his truck stood alone behind one of those sheds. I couldn't see exactly what happened, but *something* happened while the driver was gone. Because when he came back half an hour later, he resealed the doors of his container. That means someone removed the original seal, and you only do that if you want to get at the load.'

'And you think there are drugs on board the container now?' I ask.

The others are staring at me.

'Well it won't be garden gnomes,' says Wieczorkowski.

'Where exactly are you?' I ask.

'Between Dresden and Leipzig,' he says. 'I reckon we'll see you in Hamburg in four or five hours.'

'What's the haulage firm called?'

'Wellinghausen,' he says.

'We'll go straight there,' I say. 'Look after yourself. Call every half-hour. And keep your phone on; we'll try to get a fix on you, OK?'

'OK. Speak soon.'

Collective breath-holding around the table. It's as if someone has planted a bomb among us.

'Wieczorkowski is tailing a lorry that might have a load of meth or whatever for the port in Hamburg. He's near Leipzig. The lorry belongs to a haulier called Wellinghausen.'

Tschauner gets on the computer and looks up the address.

'Here,' he says. 'Wellinghausen. Got it. They're on Veddeler Damm, right next to the Köhlbrand Bridge.'

The men around the table stand up almost simultaneously and reach for their jackets.

Brux says: 'Kringe, Bartels, Tschauner, we'll go and see the haul-iers. Ms Riley, are you coming?'

I glance over at Calabretta.

He nods.

'We'll keep in touch over the day and make sure that we get some-thing going on the three murders.'

Then bam, bam, bam, we all leave the room; we all know what we have to do and where our paths are going. It's a bit like playing football for Barcelona.

On the way to the haulage firm, I call tech. They need to get a line on Wieczorkowski's mobile.

Thorsten Wellinghausen is in his mid fifties maybe, and the junior partner at the hauliers. He's wearing a brown parka over a green tweed jacket and a red-and-blue checked shirt. You can't look at him too long or it hurts your eyes.

He's standing in the yard, surrounded by an impressive fleet; next to the entrance to a large corrugated-iron hall is a small corrugated-iron kiosk where you can buy sandwiches and coffee. On offer today: ground pork and fresh onions. Not that stale onions could make it any worse.

'We mainly transport car parts from the Czech Republic,' he says; 'every day from Mladá Boleslav to the Port of Hamburg.'

'And where do the goods go from there?' asks Brux.

'All over Northern and Western Europe,' says Wellinghausen, looking round petulantly. 'What do you want from me anyway? I'm always glad to see customs on my doorstep, but I've never known the drugs squad to be interested in a heap of metal before…'

'The container was opened and resealed just before the Czech border,' I say. 'We suspect that your driver took on a load that doesn't belong in the container.'

'Why would my driver do that, if you please?' Wellinghausen wrinkles his moustache.

'Money?' suggests Tschauner.

'I pay my guys well,' Wellinghausen says. 'They don't need to do anything like that.'

'Where are the car parts loaded onto the ship?' I ask.

'At the Eurogate Terminal,' says Wellinghausen, puffing out his belly. For some reason that seems to make him proud.

Eurogate. Ha.

He probably wrestles wild animals after work.

'Can you tell us who is driving the lorry from the Czech Republic today?' asks Brux.

'I can,' says Wellinghausen, leafing through the sheets on a clipboard he's been holding the whole time.

'Alexander Jepsen,' he says. 'Family man, decent bloke. I can't imagine him getting into that kind of bullshit. Shall I phone him?'

'Definitely not,' says Brux. 'May I ask you for your telephone?'

'You can't take my phone off me.'

'I'm not taking it off you,' Brux says. 'I'm just taking it into safe keeping.'

'And I'm afraid we'll have to ask you to spend the next few hours at the police HQ,' I say, as Tschauner phones for a patrol car.

Wellinghausen gasps.

'Sorry,' I say, 'but we have to make sure nobody tips your driver off.'

'I want to speak to my lawyer at once.'

In the background, the wind sways a couple of outrageously thin birches to the right.

Industrial woodland.

Wieczorkowski is every control freak's dream – he actually rings every half hour. We know where he is all the time. At the moment, he's somewhere near Hanover.

Meanwhile we're hanging around near the motorway between the Horster Dreieck and Maschener Kreuz junctions, waiting for instructions.

I'm back in the middle of fucking nowhere. Arable farmland in Lower Saxony. Crops and fields and cows and horribly flat land as far as the eye can see.

Bartels is on the phone to the back office. After hanging up, he says: 'Alexander Jepsen has gambling debts, probably a high five-figure sum. So he could use an extra euro or two.'

'There you are,' says Brux. 'So something fits.'

On the other side of the road, a few brown and black-and-white cattle are standing by an electric fence, putting their heads together. It's an indescribably boring picture. I keep my eyes on it and notice that I'm slowly slipping into a tunnel. And with every kilometre closer Wieczorkowski gets, my tunnel stabilises.

Calabretta rings.

After a tiny moment of surprise at getting a signal in my tunnel, I answer it.

'We've found three guns in the bins in the yard behind Klatsche's cellar,' he says. 'Three small-calibre pistols with silencers and the serial numbers filed off.'

'Any other prints?'

'Loads,' he says. 'But I'm almost sure that there won't be anything we can't trace to you or Klatsche or Rocco or the three victims. Lads who use guns like that generally wear diving-suit type things to work. They don't leave traces. They're not stupid.'

I can hear him lighting a cigarette.

So I do too, because he only smokes when I do.

'Then I rang the airport and checked flights from Italy,' he says.

'Italy?' I ask.

'Call it intuition,' he says. 'It's an old mafia hitman thing to just leave the weapons at the scene. Then you can't get caught with them later.'

'And what do they say at the airport?'

'Three brothers from Catania got a plane to Hamburg yesterday evening. They're well known to our Sicilian colleagues but there's nothing definite on them. Not even mafia links.'

He drags on his cigarette and I don't take my eyes off the cows. Now they're grazing.

'The men haven't flown back yet.'

'So they're still in the country,' I say.

'Could well be,' he says; 'they might even still be in Hamburg. I've put out descriptions of them, here and across Europe. Does your Austrian have enough protection, by the way?'

'He's not *my* Austrian,' I say. 'There's a policeman sitting outside his door on the ward.'

'That won't be enough in an emergency. If a pro wants to silence an ex-pro they won't give a fuck about the police.'

'We can't station a whole century outside his door – I told him that too. It has occurred to him that things could get uncomfortable in the hospital.'

'We could get him to safety,' says Calabretta.

'A killer?' I ask.

'An informant,' says Calabretta. 'And if we can inveigle him in as a state witness, he might lead us to Gjergj Malaj.'

'Never,' I say. 'He won't blow the whistle. I'd bet my arse on it.'

'Leave your arse where it is. I'll drive round to St Georg with my guys and pick up the Austrian and our colleague from the hospital.'

'Good luck,' I say.

'When's Wieczorkowski due in Hamburg?' he asks.

'In a good hour or so.'

'Well, good luck to you too,' he says.

'Exactly,' I say and disappear back into my tunnel of chewing cows and endless waiting.

Half an hour later, Wieczorkowski calls.

'I'll be at the Horster Dreieck shortly,' he says. 'You can get moving; I'll be in touch.'

We set off. And we've just got onto the motorway, the only part of Lower Saxony that's full of people, when Calabretta rings again.

A palaver at the hospital – I can hear down the line that there's all sorts going on. The policeman outside Joe's hospital door was put out of action. Bam. Cosh to the head.

How, when and by whom, nobody quite knows.

A few minutes ago, everything was OK. Suddenly it's been knocked sideways.

'What about Joe?'

'Gone. And the wheelchair too.'

Sitting in the car with me are Brux and Tschauner. Behind us, in another car, are Kringe and Bartels.

I've put it on speaker. Brux is shaking his head and won't stop; Tschauner is staring straight ahead over the wheel and just keeps saying that it can't be true.

'Calabretta?'

'Yes?'

'Where's Faller?'

'Why?'

'Call him, please.'

I bet he won't be able to get hold of Faller.

The good thing about those American wheels is that you can get a whole heap of stuff in them.

Just as we reach the outskirts of Hamburg, I see the white Ford Transit ahead of us. Two cars in front is a container lorry. I call Wieczorkowski.

'Yes?'

'We're not far behind you,' I say; 'the dark-blue Audi.'

'Ah. Hello.'

'You all right?'

'I could do with taking a leak.'

'That's fine. We'll take over.'

'Thanks. I'll be right back.'

He heads to the nearest lay-by and we latch on to the lorry.

About ten minutes later, Wieczorkowski's behind us again. I turn round on the back seat and raise my hand in greeting. He hesitates a moment. Then he follows suit.

We drive. On and on down the overcrowded motorway.

Then here comes the port. Huge and powerful, suddenly everything around us is angular. I can see the cranes. The Köhlbrand Bridge, that old steel snake.

I've stood there some nights, wanting to jump. That was a long time ago.

The lorry indicates. Wieczorkowski phones.

'Where's he going?'

'Theoretically, he's going to the Eurogate Terminal,' I say.

But suddenly he turns off.

'He's turning off suddenly.'

'The Waltershof services,' says Tschauner, 'I bet you.'

Right. Services. A petrol station in the middle of the port area, next to a dingy transport café that's keeping its head down – kind of a filter-coffee filling station.

The lorry heads to the car park behind the café. It's not much more than a built-up lay-by really. Spattered chunks.

We park within sight.

Wieczorkowski's still on the phone. He gets out and says: 'I'll just stretch my legs.'

I look up at the sky through the car window. Dark clouds. The March day is slowly coming to an end, the light's going soft.

I watch Wieczorkowski strolling nonchalantly with his phone to his ear. Keeping an eye on the lorry. The lorry stands there. Nothing happens.

After a minute or two, Wieczorkowski comes back. Gets back into his van.

'He's waiting for someone who isn't coming.'

'We found three dealers dead this morning,' I say. 'We think they tried to mess with the big boss's deal. You know.'

'And if this driver were waiting for *those* three…' says Wieczorkowski.

'…he's probably in serious danger,' I say.

'We should get him out,' says Tschauner.

'We will get him out,' says Brux, 'but not until he's delivered the container. I want to know who else is in on it.'

He looks at me.

'OK,' I say. 'Do we step in now, or in ten minutes…? Let's wait and see what happens.'

Brux nods in satisfaction.

'The more we find out about the process, the better.'

I get out and join Wieczorkowski in the Transit. I feel better now that everyone's in a pair.

'Nice to see you,' says Wieczorkowski as I climb onto the seat beside him.

'I wasn't expecting you to pay me a visit so soon.'

'I just followed the Elbe,' he says, twinkling at me.

I didn't know people still did that. Twinkling, I mean.

But it's like so many of those odd things – this Hannes Wieczorkowski can carry it off.

The lorry judders and creeps out from behind the truck stop. I catch a brief glimpse of the driver. A man in his mid thirties with a powerful forehead and a harassed look. Alexander Jepsen.

He drives on. We follow at a slight distance. Let two cars out before we rejoin the motorway. Behind us are Brux and Tschauner in the dark-blue Audi. Then a good way behind come Kringe and Bartels in the grey Golf. We all snake along towards the Eurogate Terminal.

If anything goes wrong, there's back-up waiting round the corner – Brux was smart enough to think of that.

I'm not really the nabbing type.

It's the long straight towards the terminal. Up ahead there's the transfer point; I can already see the carriers: gantries on wheels, buzzing anxiously to and fro. Just the bones of machines driving around.

There's nothing but lorries in front and behind us now. They're tailgating. They've got no time to lose.

They're dancing to a very precisely calculated choreography, and the choreography is timed to the second.

Jepsen turns off to the right and positions his lorry at the end of a long row of trucks waiting for transhipment. We stop maybe fifty metres away, outside the site. A mosaic of colourful metallic rectangles, occasionally studded by steel struts belonging to something mobile. There are barely any people in sight – it's a world out of the belly of a factory.

I'm linked to Brux by phone; Tschauner's on the line to Kringe and Bartels.

Jepsen climbs out. He's tall and strong. Dark-blonde hair over a straight brow, three-day stubble, jumper, jeans, trucker clogs. He lights a cigarette. Wipes his hands on his trousers. Again and again.

Smoke, wipe, repeat. He appears not to have noticed us yet, although I can't actually believe that.

'He's so nervous it's not true,' says Wieczorkowski.

'I would be if I were him,' I say.

'Watch out,' says Brux down the line. 'Someone's coming.'

A man with a little gadget in his hand. Jepsen holds some papers out to him, the man scans something.

'How long do we want to wait here,' asks Wieczorkowski, as Kringe and Bartels draw up behind the dark-blue Audi in the grey Golf.

'Now,' says Brux.

We get out, Wieczorkowski, Brux, Tschauner and me; we stride over to Jepsen and his truck and the other man. They look confused when they see us. My colleagues pull out their IDs and hold them up; Brux shouts: 'Hey! Police!'

Jepsen twitches; he's clearly wondering whether to run when Kringe suddenly revs up.

I hear the Golf racing past us and Bartels yelling through the open window: 'Get down! Down! Everyone down!'

Alexander Jepsen collapses and the dock worker falls too, and I feel Wieczorkowski's big body slide to the floor past my shoulder. I slip down with him and lie protectively over him; we're lying behind the Golf, which has stopped right in front of us. Brux and Tschauner are crouching behind the car with us. I look into their eyes. They're OK. Wieczorkowski groans. Blood wells up from his shoulder under my hand.

Everyone who still can, breathes. Kringe and Bartels are lying in the car, Kringe yells that they're OK. Brux and Tschauner have their guns at the ready and a glint in their eyes; I can smell the adrenaline.

'We need an ambulance,' I say.

'You get the ambulance, I'll get the back-up,' says Brux.

We pull out our phones and call for help. Brux calls his colleagues and also orders a SWAT team and a helicopter.

'I saw him,' says Bartels, whacked, as if there were a tiger on his heels. 'He was standing on the warehouse at the back there – a guy in black with a black hood and a black gun.'

I look up to the roof, scan it with my eyes. There's nobody to be seen now.

In the container, hidden among the car parts, are a hundred kilos of uncut crystal meth. Market value in the west: about ten million euros. Headed for Stockholm. Brux has already spoken to his colleagues in Sweden.

Stuck with magnets to the bottom of the lorry are another three kilos of meth and the same amount of krok. That must be the stuff Drob, Adlo and Ronny died for.

'On principle,' says Kringe.

'Because the big guys don't let the little guys mess with their business,' says Bartels.

'Because krok is the end,' says Brux. 'That's not building a clientele, it's killing them off. You can't stand for that if you want to make long-term money from drugs.'

'Because it's all a huge pile of shit,' says Tschauner.

The ambulance has already raced off with Wieczorkowsi. The bullet passed straight through his shoulder; he's lost a lot of blood but he'll get back on his feet. The undertakers lift the lead coffins containing Jepsen and the docker into the mortuary van. Helicopters with bright searchlights keep circling the dark sky above the port. All around us there's blue light. I can hear sirens near and far.

'What is this?' I ask. 'Mexican gang warfare?'

Brux looks at me, then looks at Tschauner, who says again:

'A huge pile of shit. A stinking kingdom of filth.'

1999, New Year's Eve, just before midnight.

WIECZORKOWSKI, HANNES

I dreamt this once. Not all that long ago.

Then I thought: this is a film in my head. And suddenly things look just like that film or dream, or whatever it was.

I've followed the guy up onto the roof. I've had him in my sights for a while. And because I had no plans for tonight, and because New Year's Eve is a good evening for stake-outs because nobody's expecting you, I tailed him. The cocaine dealer.

He's the kind of guy who punches holes in his own nose as if he has a spare in the drawer. Properly off his nut, that one. Carries more and more razor blades in his pockets. Pulled one on a colleague when he went to arrest him.

When I stepped through the door onto the roof, it wasn't a razor but a gun in his hand. The gun's pointed at a man. The man's standing on the edge, his hands up.

Two steps back and he'll be over. Blood is trickling down his cheek.

Rockets shoot up on either side. Fireworks.

I pull out my gun, release the safety catch and say: Drop the weapon. Police.

The man on the edge spotted me before I said anything. Unless I'm misinterpreting his expression, he's not exactly pleased to see me. He's looking at me like my entrance has made everything worse, which I can't quite understand.

I mean – he's about to be shot.

Now he's got a chance.

Drop the weapon, I say again.

Oh sod off, punk, says the junkie and he starts laughing.

He's laughing at me. And then he starts swearing at me: Wanker, fucker, arsehole, bastard.

Does he have Tourette's?

Lousy pig, pansy, bonehead, you stink.

He's standing with an eye on each of us. The man on the edge and me.

His gun's pointed at the man who is yet to utter a word; mine's trained on him. He carries on swearing at me, but I'm not listening any more. I hear my father, who called me similar names.

Bonehead was always one of them.

Perhaps that's the word that triggers my own Tourette's. Bullet-Tourette's.

I fire off the whole clip. Until he's finally quiet, the junkie.

The man on the edge watches, at total ease.

When my clip's empty, he picks up the dead man's gun and comes towards me.

JOE (BORN: HERMANNSMEIER, JOSEF)

He actually just slams a whole round into his belly. Just flips when he's sworn at.

The cop.

And now the arsehole's lying here on the floor, not even gasping. Suddenly he's dead quiet.

Shooting the arse was meant to be my job. I had an appointment with him here, to shoot him.

He thought we were doing a drugs deal. It could have gone as smooth as silk.

But then I stuffed up. Let myself get so distracted by the razor that he managed to get my gun off me.

I knew about the razors, everyone knows, but it still confused the hell out of me.

OK, there was that razor thing in the past.

But it's got nothing to do with it. It couldn't have anything to do with it.

I lean over the arsehole, take the gun from his hand and stick it in my waistband behind my back.

That's mine, I tell the cop, and he says: Oh, right.

We'll get rid of him first, I say, and the cop says oh, right again.

We lug him down the stairs, the house is empty; tomorrow night all the dossers will be back; they'll get rid of any prints, especially with all the mud out there just now. So just keep lugging.

Keep lugging, I tell the cop and he says: I am.

And in the morning, as the arsehole sinks into the water and we're hours into the new millennium, we're still sitting in the drizzle on that bench by the dyke, looking at the Elbe and drinking gin from the petrol station, and we're not even that cold because we're pretty satisfied.

Our agreement may not be elegant, but it works.

YOU DON'T HAPPEN TO KNOW WHERE HE'S GONE?

Faller and me on the Erholung Promenade in St Pauli. We're smoking and drinking coffee from paper cups. The jetties are below us. A few ships, a few tourists, a lot of gulls. No sun in the sky.

'Did the gentlemen from Catania ever turn up again?' asks Faller.

I shake my head. 'No news as yet,' I say. 'There's an international warrant out. But you know how it goes with people like that.'

He nods. 'I know.'

He watches a gull.

'And why was there a sniper on the container terminal?'

'We think Malaj's behind it all,' I say.

'Well, well,' says Faller, giving me a disconnected look.

'And he's not stupid. Wednesday night there was a drugs raid in a little club; the next morning, three dealers were dead. Anyone wanting to do his thing at the container port would have to reckon with us appearing to screw it up.'

'You certainly screwed it up. And at least there were no people in the container, only drugs.'

He's right there.

'Unfortunately, everyone who could have talked is now dead,' I say.

'Which explains the sniper, of course,' says Faller.

I watch the clouds as they split and join up and push into each other. As if they wanted to build a world of their own up there.

'The guys turned the whole port upside down over night,' I say. 'No trace of him. As if he was never even there.'

Down on the water, the harbour police race by in one of their antiquated boats. With their Lego cutesiness and framed by the much-photographed jetties, they always look like they've just tumbled out of an early-evening TV series.

'How's our colleague from Leipzig?' asks Faller.

'Doing OK. But he lost a lot of blood.'

'Is he responsive?'

'Not really, not yet,' I say. 'Why?'

'Just wondered.'

Faller sips at his coffee, sticks out his bottom lip and nods, tortoise-like.

'The only person who can still be a danger to Malaj is Joe,' I say, thinking that that's not true, because Wieczorkowski knows about Joe's bank box. And so do I. But there's no way in hell I'm discussing that with Faller.

Faller raises his eyebrows and says: 'Hmm. Unfortunately, Joe's disappeared.'

'And you don't happen to know where he's gone?' I ask.

Faller tilts his head to the left, then to the right. 'Nope.'

'Come on, Faller.'

'He's not stupid either, my girl. He knows that if the worst comes to the worst, he's next on the list. If a deal's gone wrong for someone like Malaj and he has to tidy up, then he really tidies up. And if Joe's as smart as I think he is, he's long gone, back to the Carinthian Alps to enjoy the spring sunshine.'

'In plaster, or what?'

I wonder whether Faller knows about the bank box. He scratches his chin, drinks a gulp of coffee and says nothing more.

The sun pops out from behind the clouds, casts its rays over the Elbphilharmonie; the clouds gather again, and the big box of a building, whose job it is – or at least is meant to be – to beam light right across this town, just eats up the sunshine.

Among foes and among friends.

MALAJ GJERGJ

Oh they were as happy as Larry.

They're happy as Larry about every penny they can take off me. And of course, for people like that, ten million's a lot of money.

For me: bummer.

The business with the containers was low risk.

It would have been good.

For my cousin in Stockholm it's a real bummer.

Now he's empty-handed. He'll have to think of something else.

I'm out. Next week I'm buying that hotel complex in Bulgaria.

Nice.

Black Sea.

Five Stars.

Deluxe.

There are two lorries already heading that way from the Czech Republic. My cousin from Sofia is coming specially to settle everything. Then he'll invest the money right back into the hotel.

Up and running.

Who gives a shit about the Hamburgers and their measly container port?

FALLER, GEORG

So I said to my wife, what do you think? Shall we head to the mountains again this summer?

HERMANNSMEIER, JOSEF

Bit dark down here in the cellar. But the sky outside is getting brighter every day. And the bed is good.

My bones are healing.

I bet the woman can't stand me. She's given me a cat mug.

FLOODLIGHT
(Four weeks later)

Yesterday, spring arrived. All of a sudden it's seventeen degrees, and I swear tomorrow every tree will be in blossom.

Faller and I are sitting outside a café on the pavement in the sun with our backs to the tentatively warmed wind. Right in front of us, a surfer is liberating his greying Fiat Ducato from the moss that's grown on the car over the winter.

I order a latte in a glass, Faller orders an espresso. And a lemonade. 'With lemon, please.'

He blinks towards the sky and says: 'I just read in the paper what happened in the Santa Fu. Jeeze. Those poor kids.'

'I know,' I say.

There was a delivery of krok for Hamburg that did arrive. It must have belonged with the crystal in the Graciosa Bar. Now we know who the krok was aimed at. Or – to put it another way – where the target group is.

In prison.

It seems like the whole load ended up in the Fuhlsbüttel Young Offenders Institution. And they swallowed it whole.

Now they're all detoxing and suffering and downing morphine together; the local paper ran a big front-page story about the 'RUSSIAN JAIL DRUG' today.

The waitress brings our drinks, Faller smiles rather too suavely for my taste. He's sold the Pontiac. I don't know if that'll do him any good.

He sniffs his espresso, closes his eyes, takes a hot sip, sniffs again and says: 'Aah.'

Once he's drunk the coffee, he turns his attention to the lemonade. Starts by taking out the slice of lemon and eating it.

'Aah,' again.

Then he drinks the yellow liquid a sip at a time and it seems to make him disproportionately happy.

'Are you starting a new drinks fetish?' I ask.

'No,' he says. 'I'm just fasting.'

'You're fasting?'

Faller's never gone four hours without eating as long as I've known him. Two hours, really. And even then, not without the occasional currywurst.

'I need an internal cleansing, my girl.'

He waves to the waitress. 'Could I have a glass of water with lemon too, please?'

Internal cleansing?

Something bothers me about that.

'I've been meaning to ask: have you heard from Joe?' I say.

He looks at me with that expression that men learn very young and never unlearn: in one ear and out the other. I'm not remotely interested in what you just said.

I try to look back just as indifferently, but it's a bit like looking at the TV test card.

I was on the phone to Wieczorkowski yesterday. He's not back at work yet, much to his annoyance. He says he'll start climbing the walls soon. And he's got time to mull over theories about Joe's disappearance. Either, Wieczorkowski says, Joe really did make it home to the mountains and is playing at being Heidi's grandpa. Or else he went on a big harbour tour and is lying at the bottom of the North Sea in concrete boots.

'Couldn't he still be in Hamburg?' I asked.

'You're offended because he didn't say goodbye to you.'

'Nonsense,' I said. 'It's just that I can't stop thinking about the man, same as you. And his bloody bank box in Switzerland.'

'There is no bank box now,' Wieczorkowski said.

'Why do you say that?'

'You don't think he trusts us, do you? You're not thinking about that bank box because you want to leave it in peace, are you?'

That comes to mind as I slip deeper and deeper into the Faller stare. And I wonder who *I* can actually trust.

It's still not completely dark; there's still a strip of light on the western horizon. But the floodlights are on already, and they're on in people's heads too, because FC St Pauli has brought in a new coach for the end of the season. An old Marxist with a good brain and a big heart and a legendary thigh injury. Everyone's happy when a guy like that arrives. The right man for the relegation battle. But it feels like we're always in the relegation battle.

A relegation battle like that doesn't make me nervous.

What makes me nervous is not standing in my spot in the south stand fan block.

I'm sitting in a VIP box.

The head of security here is marrying Faller's daughter in two months, and that's why we're all invited. Faller, Calabretta, Schulle, Brückner, Rocco and Carla and Klatsche and me, and a few other people I don't know – friends of Faller's son-in-law-to-be. We asked Brux and Tschauner too, but they support HSV.

Which is fair enough.

So now we're sitting in these weird seats, which is all wrong 'cos we ought to be standing. But if you want to invite someone to a St Pauli match, then it has to be in the VIP boxes. Because they're empty.

The stands are all full.

Absolutely jam-packed solid.

So I'm sitting. And watching. And I don't feel right.

And I keep finding myself thinking about the graffiti that someone sprayed on a house wall round the corner from me:

'Where's the VIP lounge now, you cunts?'

Here, people; the lounge is here. Please don't hate me for it. It's almost kick-off. We're waiting for you.

Here they come.

I look at the players and have the feeling, yet again, that they're getting younger every week.

They start running and jostling and jumping and tackling; they let themselves get hemmed in and break out and win corners and none of it achieves anything much, and after just twenty minutes they're hoofing it long.

I'm not angry with them. I know what it's like. Anyway, it's not a proper match for me today. Because we're sitting down.

Klatsche's sitting next to me. He's starting to get better. He closed his bar for a couple of weeks and took care of his gran instead of the nightlife. He says she needs it more than all the rest right now. And he says he needs a fresh start. So tomorrow he wants to begin with a bit of renovating. We've bought blue paint. I said: But I'll paint the cellar.

I keep taking his hand. You know, just between beers.

On my other side, a young woman is sliding around in her seat. She has blonde hair piled up in a bun; a heavy fringe falls into her face. She looks very friendly; there are some people whose eyes are always smiling. She's holding a glass of white wine in her hand, and when our eyes meet for the third or fourth time, she raises her glass and says: 'Silvaner.'

I raise my Astra and say: 'Beer.'

'No,' she says, 'this is Riesling. I'm Silvana.'

I say 'Oh' and 'Sorry', and then she laughs and I laugh too, and now it's official – all I can think of is booze.

Probably I need a fresh start too.

And maybe a fresh coat of paint.

Carla and Rocco are sitting behind me, having a whale of a time.

'Hi, Beer. Such a pretty name.'

I shrug.

'You guys can call me what you like.'

Sometimes all I can do is shake my head over myself. So I give the first half up as a bad lot, and stop pretending to concentrate in the forty-fourth minute. Carla always calls this kind of thing a 'hard-fought bugger all'.

Then it's half-time.

The stadium announcer is standing in the middle, talking.

About a charity thing.

They like to do charity at half-time.

I'm still not quite all there.

They can do Chastity at half-time too, I think, and even I don't know which drawer I pulled that out from, and then I think I must be cracking up.

Standing in the centre circle is Gjergj Malaj.

His brother's there too. The classy brother who used to run his slightly less classy businesses for him.

They're actually standing there, both of them, the two best organised criminals in this city, or maybe even the whole of Germany, handing out cheques for nurseries for special-needs kids.

We all sit stock still in our VIP box.

Nobody says a thing. But the rage is with us. Hanging like an oozing red mass over our heads.

Schulle lets a little air through his teeth; it's like a hissing from another dimension.

This doesn't seem to bother anyone else in the stadium.

They're clapping or not listening or singing the same song for the hundredth time.

'I've got to get out of here,' I say and stand up, and at that precise moment, shots are fired, barely audible, and the Albanian and his brother topple over.

One.

Two.

Lights out.

They have little red holes in their foreheads.

Nobody's clapping any more.

Except Faller.

He claps slowly and dreamily, as if someone's just played a particularly enchanting melody that really spoke to his heart.

Everyone else is screaming.

'Faller,' I say, watching one of the empty VIP boxes above the stadium's south stand. Someone just moved up there. Stiff and spectral, but I saw it.

'Faller, how did he get up there? He's not even out of the wheelchair yet.'

Faller doesn't look at me. He stares into space. His world seems to have switched into slow motion. There are the merest hints of tears in his eyes, but he doesn't look remotely sad.

'Faller,' I say again, 'how the hell did he get up there?'

'I really couldn't tell you,' says Faller, and he stands up, pulls his hat over his brow and leaves.

Calabretta lights a cigarette.

THANKS

Nora Mercurio, Suhrkamp Verlag.

Karen Sullivan (for her courage) and West Camel, Orenda Books.

Rachel Ward for her loving translation, and for saving and transforming the sound.

Katy Derbyshire, because she said: 'Do it.'

Tom Bernhardt of the State Criminal Investigation Office, Saxony, Holger Vehren of Hamburg Police, Christian Meinhold of the federal police in Pirna and Johann Pechthold from the Dresden customs office.

Rico Hanke, Nicole and Robin Schulz, Dorthe Hansen, Christian Sobiella, Kerstin Busse and Gitta Ohlsen-Vongehr.

The Kurhaus in general and Silvana, Babsi, Markus, Gunther, Christoph and Daniel in particular.

And of course Domenico, Rocco and my parents, because they keep putting up with it and making time for me.

***

The quotation from Arthur Fellig was taken from *Weegee's New York, Reportagen eines legendären Photographen, 1935–1960* (Schirmer/Mosel, 2000). English version: *Weegee: The Autobiography (Annotated),* (Devault-Graves Digital Editions, 2013)